REVENGE

OF THE

RED SQUARE

Also by The Penny Brothers

The Golden Pig

REVENGE

OF THE

RED SQUARE

THE PENNY BROTHERS

Matador
9 Priory Business Park
Kibworth Beauchamp
Leicestershire LE8 0RX, UK
Tel: (+44) 116 279 2299
Fax: (+44) 116 279 2277
Email: books@troubador.co.uk
Web: www.troubador.co.uk/matador

ISBN 9781780880686

British Library Cataloguing in Publication Data.
A catalogue record for this book is available from the British Library.

Typeset in 11pt Bembo by Troubador Publishing Ltd, Leicester, UK
Printed and bound in the UK by TJ International, Padstow, Cornwall

Matador is an imprint of Troubador Publishing Ltd

For Harvey, wherever he is.

Part One

A strange way to make a living

In the leafy garden of a 1950's semi in Cricklewood, *The Amazing Harvey*, as he was professionally known, prepared to entertain an attentive and appreciative party of wide-eyed children. That, at least, was the theory. He stood at the far end of the immaculate lawn, past the potting shed by the strawberry beds, footling around with his props in the fruitless hope that his assistant, Boltini, would arrive in time to draw fire from the kids from hell. If the guy was half cut again, he'd have his guts for garters.

He'd never had much luck with assistants; the Lovely Leanne had run off with the man with the squint from the Job Centre while they were resting between bookings; the Daring Denise had broken her leg on the ski-slopes of Val Doonican or some such far flung resort, and Sharon had jacked it all in for the mystic allure of stacking supermarket shelves in West Croydon. Finally, he'd decided to get a male assistant, and *this* was the result; standing around in a field in Cricklewood waiting for pisshead to arrive. His real name was James Bolton - hence Boltini - and he'd seemed so promising at the start, when he ran into him behind the bar at *The Dog and Duck*, doing occasional card tricks for the punters. No wonder the guy had agreed to work for peanuts, when he wasn't monkeying around he was practically useless.

The lady of the house, Mrs Olga Flanagan, heiress to a Russian-Irish shipping tycoon, sailed down the path with an imperious air like a pocket battleship on manoeuvres. She had no time for children's entertainers, having always found something deeply suspect about men in their mid-forties who made a living from wearing fancy dress and deceiving minors.

"Well, Mr Harvey?"

"Just call me *Amazing.*"

She arched an eyebrow in disbelief. "Have it your own way, but the children are getting restless," she said. "I think you should begin."

Harvey cast a last forlorn glance down the garden for Boltini, then resigned himself to his fate. He wouldn't have minded so much but he needed an assistant to divert the audience's attention away from his woeful performance.

"Can I have the money *now?*" he asked sheepishly.

"Surely it's customary to pay *after* the performance," she said.

"Not for me. The number of times I've worked for nothing…" Mrs Flanagan looked concerned. "…is few and far between," he added hastily, "but I do like to be sure of getting paid. I'd hate to have to drop by one night and turn your car into a heap of manure."

Two pencilled eyebrows were raised in mounting concern.

"Look, your money's safe in this envelope," said Mrs Flanagan, retrieving exhibit A from her cardigan sleeve, like a white rabbit from a hat. "There's nothing to worry about. You do the show, you get paid and you leave. Simple."

"Great," he said, without conviction. He walked back up the lawn to his makeshift stage, where a group of hyperactive eight-year-olds were beginning to disassemble some of his props with vandal-like glee.

Harvey tugged at the cuffs of his jacket and cleared his throat.

"Ladies, gentlemen, children… well, children, anyway. Prepare to be astonished, prepare to be astounded, prepare to have your faculties disconfabulated, discombobulated and disconfusticated as I mesmerise you with the magical, mystical enchantments of a thousand ages of wizardry. Way back in the mists of time… I tell a lie, it was last Tuesday."

He paused for the laughter that never came. Someone at the back of the audience blew a raspberry.

Harvey looked up with ill-concealed irritation. An anaemic youth with wire-framed glasses, an electric yellow tee shirt bearing the letter 'B' in fluorescent red and a purple cape appeared at his shoulder.

"Boltini, where the h…eck have you been?"

The assistant took an early bow, tripped over his untied shoelaces and fell headlong into the props so meticulously arranged on the magician's stage table. Rising unsteadily to his feet, Boltini made his way shakily past the potting shed and was violently ill in the strawberry beds.

Fourteen eight-year-olds laughed like drains, poked each other in the ribs and pointed at the less than magical figure of Boltini as he returned to join his mentor. Mrs Flanagan, meanwhile, bore a striking resemblance to a battleship which had come under fire in the midships and knew exactly what to do about it.

Harvey blundered on.

"Thank you most kindly. I appear before you today fresh from a thrilling expedition to the mythical isle of Maroonga, a voyage blessed with the discovery of a positive plethora of new and astounding tricks. As I'm sure you will know, on the isle of Maroonga, *everyone* is a magician and they have normal people like yourselves to entertain them. Why? I hear you ask. Well, it's a strange and mystical place. They all sit around in deckchairs wearing big hats and playing the bongos while watching people making tea and crumpets."

"Get on with it, mister. Do a trick or summat," chivvied an exasperated eight-year-old in the front row, whose patience had been sorely tested.

There's always one, isn't there, thought Harvey.

"Why are we waiting? Why are we waiting?" sang a boy with goofy teeth, in a tuneless wail.

Or two…

"Come on granddad, are you a magician or wot?" cried the teenager from next door, who had been standing on an old tea chest to see over the hedge. "This show's not even worth gate-crashing!"

But when it gets to three, thought Harvey, then it's definitely time to…

"Go!" shouted Mrs Flanagan. "And never darken my yew again." Harvey had been about to pack up his remaining props and beat a hasty retreat, when he suddenly realised that she was talking to the interloper from next door. At least that was the only inference he *could* draw from the sight of the stately Mrs Flanagan flinging a moth-eaten old tennis ball at the hedge.

"Thank you, thank you," he resumed. "Now without further ado, let me show you a miraculous card trick I learned from Houdini." Harvey reached into his trouser pocket and pulled out a deck of Bicycle playing cards. As he did so the packet opened, spilling half of them onto the floor.

"Surely he was an escapologist?" queried Mrs Flanagan, as the children began to laugh like a pack of hyenas at the collapse of the trick.

"Ah, no, I meant Sid Houdini, Harry's brother's grandson," said Harvey vaguely, as he tried to pick up as many cards as he could. "Now then, which of these delightful children is the birthday boy or girl?"

"Go on, Sophie, stand up," said the boy with the buck teeth.

A sweet little girl with her hair in bunches stood up.

"Happy Birthday, Sophie," said Harvey. "How old are you?"

"Eight."

"You know, I was *ate* once… by a lion at the circus, but the ringmaster cracked his whip and it spat me out in the nick of time," said Harvey.

Sophie smiled, in a vain attempt to humour the funny man, who was obviously nuts.

"Pick a card, any card," continued Harvey, offering a woefully small selection of playing cards to the little girl. Shyly, she took one and held it to her chest.

Harvey closed his eyes and walked clockwise in a circle three

4

times. He put his hand to his forehead, feeling giddy. He'd forgotten to say the magic words! They could kick you out of the Magic Triangle for a lesser offence, if you were in it to begin with. Perhaps they wouldn't notice. He closed his eyes and put his finger tips to his temples. He was getting a migraine.

"It can only be the...eight of clubs. Am I right?"

Sophie looked at her card in confusion.

"I don't know, mister, I don't play cards, but it's got a funny man on with a curly hat."

"It's the joker, how apt," said Mrs Flanagan.

"That would have been my second choice," he said, hurriedly taking the card back from the little girl and placing it in his pocket. He lifted his collapsible hat from the props table, tapped it twice with his wand and the hat opened out with a pop. He just needed a distraction other than the sight of Boltini vomiting in different parts of the garden. He placed the hat on his head and smiled what he hoped was a winning smile.

"Now, who can tell me what a magician keeps in his hat? Can anyone? Mrs Flanagan?"

"In your case I'd hesitate to guess," she replied, frostily.

"Sandwiches?" wondered a boy in the second row.

"Chocolate biscuits?" asked Sophie.

"Cake!" cried another, as the food motif took hold.

The children had begun to lose interest and started picking their noses or dead-heading Mrs Flanagan's prize petunias. The boy with the goofy teeth was clearly in need of the toilet.

"Good ideas but not the right answer I'm afraid. Shall we see?" added the magician. He lifted his hat to reveal a small and terrified white mouse. A couple of the girls screamed and the mouse took off like a rocket down the garden.

"This," said Harvey, gesticulating at the recently vacated space, "is Rover." He looked inside his hat in the vague hope of locating the rodent, but further probing of the top of his head revealed only a small pile of moist mouse droppings. At least he finally had their attention.

"Where's he gone, mister?" asked Sophie.

"Don't worry, kids, I expect he felt like a bit of exercise. It's quite cramped in my hat so he probably came over a bit faint. He suffers from claustrophobia you know." He was babbling; he often did when there was nothing useful left to say. It was better than admitting that his act was a shambolic farce and that he should have stuck to teaching.

"Boltini! We have a mouse missing! There…over by the shed, quickly, get him, now!"

Boltini stared at him, green to the gills, with a look of sullen defiance on his pale yet uninterested face.

"The name's James, mate, and sod this for a game of soldiers!" he said, walking off towards the house and his transport out of there.

"You'll never work in show business again!" called Harvey, after him.

Another raspberry wafted on the breeze, this time from Boltini. "I should have listened to them all," said the disgruntled assistant aloud as he slouched off. "Never work with children or animals. Only there's a third category to watch out for…pillocks called *The Amazing Harvey*!"

Sweat broke out along Harvey's hairline. Disaster loomed. He was reminded of his first professional engagement – 'The Mendelssohn Job' – when everything that *could* go wrong *had* gone wrong, resulting in the end of his career as far as Hendon, Golders Green and Finchley were concerned. In retrospect, it had been a walk in the park compared with *this*.

"Ladies, gentlemen, children… the kid with the goofy teeth, I'd like to say what a fantastic audience you've been…I, I …" he looked around him for inspiration, but none was forthcoming. He felt like he was stranded in a wilderness of despair and all hope was lost.

"You're rubbish at magic, mister," said a girl with ginger hair and freckles. "Your assistant threw up, your mouse ran off and you don't even know any card tricks. I'd give up if I were you."

Mrs Flanagan looked at him with a combination of disappointment, annoyance and pity and returned the envelope she had been holding for safe keeping to her handbag.

"Out of the mouths of babes," she said.

Harvey opened his jacket to see if he still had anything left up his sleeve and was met by the flutter of wings and a face full of flying feathers as Maurice, his white dove, made a bid for freedom. Flying off into the wide blue yonder, Maurice dropped a message from on high, all down Harvey's shirt front. It seemed profoundly symbolic.

The children hooted with laughter. This guy may be a rotten magician but he was a master of chaos and failure.

"Can you do balloon animals?" asked the kid with the buck teeth, on the basis that if they tried long enough they might be able to find *something* Harvey could do.

For the first time, *The Amazing Harvey* seemed to get really pissed off.

"Do balloon animals?! What do you take me for? I'm an artiste, not some drongo who ties *balloons* into funny shapes! I don't have a big red nose and long flapping boots, do I? No, I ruddy don't. Look, has anybody got any pets?" he asked.

"I've got a gerbil at home," said the girl with the ginger hair. "Timmy, his name is."

"What bloody good is *that!*" snapped Harvey. "I'm looking for an animal I can use in my act; a cat from Cricklewood, not a terrapin from Timbuktu!"

The girl started sobbing uncontrollably and Mrs Flanagan fixed him with an icy stare until he was forced to apologise.

"Sorry, young lady. I do apologise, it's just that as you may have noticed, one or two things have gone a little wrong with the act today so I was hoping to show you some *real* magic to make up for it." He smiled to hide the pain.

"I've got a goldfish called Sammy," said Sophie, quietly. "Would he be any good?"

"Yes! Brilliant! Thank you, Sophie," said the magician. "Would you go and fetch him for me, please."

As she walked off up to the house, the long lank figure of Boltini shuffled back towards the party.

"I knew you wouldn't desert the act, Boltini," said Harvey. "One day all of this will be yours," he said, gesturing grandiosely at the tatty collection of broken props. "All you need to do is fetch Maurice down off the neighbour's roof and track down Rover, and we're back in business."

Boltini looked at Harvey with a pained expression. "Has anyone seen the keys to my van?" he asked aloud, to no one in particular.

"Now, kids, while Sophie goes off to get the goldfish let me entertain you with some juggling. I used to do this in the circus you know," said Harvey.

"What happened?" asked Mrs Flanagan, out of morbid curiosity. "Are they still in business?"

Harvey picked up three patchwork juggling balls and threw them into the air, one after the other until they formed a flying circle. Boltini wandered back over to the strawberry beds to see if he could locate his keys among the vomit spattered plants.

"Oh, yes. Uncle Henry's Flying Circus, it was called. We toured Army bases mainly."

"Poor devils," added Olga Flanagan, "dodging bullets all day and being forced to watch your act when they got back."

"This is rotten," said the kid with the buck teeth. "All you've done is lose things and a juggling trick my dad could do."

Harvey's self-confidence finally seemed to desert him. He was on the verge of throwing in the towel when Sophie returned with a goldfish in a bowl.

"Ah, yes, but can your father do *this*?" said Harvey, taking the bowl. His juggling balls hit the ground unheeded.

He took a large red handkerchief from an inside jacket pocket and draped it over the goldfish bowl. The audience fell silent. Even Boltini, who had been moping around looking for his keys, paused momentarily to watch and marvel. He hadn't seen this trick before.

"The illusion I am about to perform is technically impossible," said Harvey.

He lifted the hankie and removed the fish from the bowl with his hand. He placed it into a large brown paper bag and blew into the bag until it was fully inflated. Holding it out in front of him, Harvey passed his left hand over the top of the bag and recited the familiar incantation, "Hocus Pocus, fish-bones choke us." Then he placed the bag on the table in front of him and hit it three times with a wooden mallet. The silence deepened into a deathly hush. You could have heard a gnat fart.

Harvey picked up the paper bag and peered anxiously inside.

"And that, as they say, is magic!" he cried. "You've been a wonderful audience, thank you and goodbye!"

He fixed Boltini with a knowing look. "Here are your keys," he said, "get the stuff and meet me at the van in five," he added, legging it for the garden gate.

"Oi, mister, where's the fish?" asked the kid with the buck teeth.

"I'm sorry, I'm a magician, not a pet shop owner," said Harvey over his shoulder as he vanished.

Part Two

Meanwhile somewhere in North London

In the ill-kempt offices of *JP Confidential, Private Investigators to the Stars,* Hymie Goldman and Mike Murphy sat amid the clutter with sour expressions, drinking a murky brown liquid. It was a substance whose composition had long since baffled the finest forensic scientists of NW3 and was known to habitués of the Black Kat café as 'coffee'. Certainly a medium sized dose precluded sleep for several days and had been known to stun an adult male gorilla but when you'd said that, you'd said everything.

"How's the case going, Goldman?" asked Mike; the primate in question.

"I presume you're referring to the *new* case, Mike?"

"Well, I wasn't asking after your luggage, mate."

"The only baggage I have to lug around is you, Murphy. As for the case, it's too early to tell."

"Is there any money in it?"

"Mike, if there wasn't, I wouldn't be wasting my time, would I?"

"I hope not, Goldman, but you're not even the best businessman at this end of the Finchley Road. I wouldn't trust your business nous as far as I could throw it. What's the client called anyway? You're being very secretive about the whole case."

"Secretive? Pah! It's just that I have to respect client confidentiality."

"I'm not buying it, mate. Who's your client?"

"Mr Redrum," said Hymie, quietly.

"Mr who?"

"Redrum," repeated Hymie.

"That's the name of a horse, you wally. You haven't gone and got mixed up with the county set again, have you? After all the trouble we had last time. Are you mad?"

"Look, Mike, this is why I didn't tell you about the case, because I knew you'd jump to conclusions, wrong conclusions. It's about the only exercise your feeble mind gets these days. Okay, so it sounds dodgy. No one's called Mr Redrum. That's why I'm trying to find out how much baloney this guy's feeding me before I get in too deep. So how are tricks with you, my massive chum? Heard from the bird in Blackpool?"

Mike fell silent and took another sip of coffee. He winced.

"No, and I don't want to talk about it."

"I've always said women are a curse," said Hymie, insensitively. "They bat their eyelashes at you, you fall like a ton of bricks and then they hang you out to dry. It's only a question of time. Been there, done that, got the tee shirt," he concluded.

"I never met your wife, did I, Goldman. Were you in love?"

"It was a long time ago," said Hymie. "Some things are best left in the past."

"Was she a looker?"

"As I said, it's best left in the past," repeated Hymie.

"I'll take that as a 'no' then. Did it hurt when she left you?" continued Mike.

"Blunt as a badger's bum, aren't you, Murphy. I don't need a bloody psychiatrist or a shoulder to cry on. I get along fine without all that hearts and flowers crap, so just leave it out. And if this is another diversion to stop me asking about *your* caseload, think again, mate. Come on, how many new clients have you got?"

"Plenty, mate, plenty. I'm a client magnet. Ask Janie. Come to think of it, where is Janie?"

"Family funeral, I thought," said Hymie. "Her Uncle Len died."

"No, can't be," said Mike. "She hasn't got an Uncle Len. Besides, she hasn't been in for weeks, just look at the dust on those files."

"I wondered why everything was in such a mess," continued Hymie, "but without Janie to point it out to me, it didn't really register."

"Maybe she had a better offer?" said Mike. "She is the best personal assistant we've ever had."

"What? A better offer than JP Confidential? No, she'll have been kidnapped or won the National Lottery or something. We should call the police," said Hymie, impulsively. "No, on second thoughts..." he added hastily.

"Have you heard anything of Inspector Decca lately?" asked Mike. "He was your best buddy in Blackpool. It's funny how he's disappeared since we got back."

"It's like you said, Mike; what happened in Blackpool stays in Blackpool. Now, you call the agency about a new receptionist cum bottle-washer, while I go and earn the dosh to keep us afloat."

"That'll be the day, Goldman," said Mike, heading for the peace and quiet of his own office to make some calls.

Part Three

Detective-u-[don't]-like

What *had* happened to Inspector Ray Decca? Did anyone know? Did anyone care? The *nearly* man of the Metropolitan Constabulary had seemed to be on the verge of total meltdown twelve months earlier, but after a short stay at a rest home for retired loonies in Blackpool, he'd suddenly become a completely different man. Once he'd been a workaholic with a cast iron commitment to the job, but after the collapse of his marriage, the promotion above him of a host of lesser men and the realisation that even terminal loser, Hymie Goldman, seemed to have a more successful career, he had ceased to give a damn.

On his return to active service they'd put him in charge of the unsolved cases unit and assigned his arch-nemesis, Sergeant Barry Terse, to work for him on the basis that sometimes two wrongs could make a right. Besides, even if they didn't, it surely made sense to bury the two least popular officers on the force in a small room in the bowels of HQ with a bunch of cases no one wanted to hear any more about.

Decca sat behind his grey desk in a room no bigger than a portable toilet, poring over the crossword in *The Hendon Herald*. "Large flightless bird? Three letters? Sounds like the ex-wife! No, wait, it's on the tip of my tongue."

The grey phone on his desk trilled uncharacteristically in the land that time forgot. He lifted the receiver out of idle curiosity.

13

"Hello, Ray Decca."

"Oh hello, mate. Your ex-wife said I should give you a call. I'm trying to get the sports channel on your old satellite service and it keeps on coming up with an error message. Any ideas?"

"Who is this?" asked Decca, incredulously.

"Chaz Dipswell, I'm your ex's new partner."

"Well, Mr Dipstick, I suggest you take the remote…"

"Yeees."

"Press the red button three times…"

"Yeees."

"And shove it right up your arse. Good day to you!"

He slammed down the receiver. The nerve of some people. As if it wasn't bad enough that his marriage was over, his career in tatters and when he wasn't working in a portaloo, he was living in a bedsit above the dry cleaners off Hendon Broadway; somehow everyone seemed to think that he should be perfectly happy with his lot.

As Decca sat seething, the door flew open as if propelled by a hurricane, and the excitable figure of Sergeant Barry Terse appeared like a dustbowl twister, clutching a file.

"Whatever happened to knocking, Terse?"

"It's still going strong, sir. There are knocking shops everywhere."

"Har, ruddy har, Terse. Why are you so upbeat today?"

"We've got a new case, Chief."

"Oh, just bung it over there with the stale doughnuts, Terse. I'm on my tea-break."

"Yes, sir, but it's a real *live* case."

"Look, Terse…Barry, we're still only half way through 2002. I'm hardly likely to get excited about a new case from 2003, am I?"

"No, Chief, a *real* case. A homicide," persisted the sergeant.

"Terse, calm down. Let's get a reality check here; is that a flying pig I can see through the air vent? Who on earth would put *us* in charge of a homicide investigation? Has the whole force contracted beri beri or something?"

"Well, sir, it's only a goldfish homicide, but it's a step in the right direction, isn't it."

Decca banged his head on the desk in front of him then regretted the gesture.

"Are you taking the piss, Terse?"

"No, sir, Lord Tom O'Connor…"

"The guy who chairs the Police Complaints Authority?" interjected Decca.

"Yeah, well, his granddaughter was having a kid's party at home in Cricklewood, when the magician they'd hired killed her goldfish then scarpered."

"And they want us to investigate it?"

"That's about the size of it, sir," concluded Terse.

"And this is your idea of a golden opportunity? A case that clearly no one else will touch with a bargepole because it's a bad joke and if we can't crack it we'll be hauled up in front of a complaints enquiry?"

"Now that you mention it, sir, perhaps it's not a step in the right direction, after all."

"No, Terse. Come back 2002, all is forgiven."

"Yes, sir."

"Do we have any choice in the matter, Sergeant?"

"What do you think, sir?"

"I suspected as much. Ah well, it will be good to get out into the daylight again, I keep feeling like I'm working in a cinema. See if you can get us a car, Terse."

"Will do, Chief," said the sergeant, backing out of the room.

Part Four

Conspiracy Theories R Us

It was a long way back from Cricklewood to anywhere, when all your magic tricks had gone wrong, you'd killed an innocent goldfish belonging to the girl whose party you'd been performing at and her mother hadn't paid you. *The Amazing Harvey* had never felt less able to live up to his billing. Even his assistant, Boltini, driving them back to Golders Green in the Magic Wagon, a purple Ford Transit with a giant rabbit painted on the side and a six foot wand stuck on the roof, seemed sullen and resentful. He'd have driven off and left him there if Harvey hadn't taken the keys to the van.

"Look, Harvey, no offence, mate, but you're rubbish. Really bad. You have to be the worst magician I've ever seen. And I'm your *assistant*... so, what does that make me? *Understudy* to the world's worst magician? Do you think I like following you around with a dustpan and brush? Do I look like a terminal masochist?"

Harvey looked at him dejectedly in silence for a while. "Et tu, brute," just about summed up how he felt. When the whole world was against you, all you needed was a friend and confidante to stab you in the back.

"Listen, Jack,"

"James!" cried Boltini, irritably.

"Jack, James, whatever...we all have bad days. Don't you ever have them? You could have fooled me anyway, you looked like a bag of shit when you turned up at that party. I may not be the best magician in the world, but at least I take the act seriously. I'm always well turned out."

"Frequently turfed out!" snapped Boltini, resentful of such a gross slur on his professionalism. He swerved to avoid a traffic bollard. "I've always given the act 110% myself," he added.

"So have I!" snapped Harvey.

"Yeah, well, I just think that we should have more to show for 220% effort than a bunch of testimonials ending in 'off', don't you, Harvey? We didn't even get paid I take it?"

"I was *that* close," said Harvey, holding up his right index finger and thumb, pressed tightly together. "The old battleaxe even showed me the envelope with the cash in to whet my appetite."

"I'll take that as a 'no' then."

The van pulled up outside 18 Elmcroft Avenue and Boltini switched off the engine.

"I'm sorry, Bolters old chap," continued Harvey. "Come in and have a drink, there's something I want to talk to you about," he added.

Boltini wondered if he was trying to tell him that the act was over. Surely that was worth talking about, if only to confirm it was true. They got out and walked down the path. The house was easily the scruffiest in the road. Its facade seemed nearly as shambolic as its latest tenant. Inside, everything was scattered indiscriminately as though a particularly untidy burglar had been looking for valuables amidst a giant haystack of dross. In fact it always looked that way.

The only possessions Harvey owned with any discernible value were a cast bronze statuette of the Magic Triangle's first president, Derek Deviant, playing with his balls, which now adorned the grotty sideboard and an original advertising poster from the 1920's for one of the greats of stage magic. Boltini eyeballed it as he passed.

"Is that a genuine Po?" he asked.

Harvey followed his glance.

"No, even better, a genuine Pong," he said absently.

"Never heard of him. No, wait; it says Ying Tong Pong, the famous Chinese magician. I thought it was Po, not Pong," said Boltini.

"He was originally billed as *The Mighty Pong*, but soon learnt to his cost that his posters were more likely to attract the attention of the local public health inspector than the throngs of cheering crowds he craved, so he changed his name to Ying Tong Po and never looked back. You've probably heard the story of how he died on stage?" said Harvey.

"Tough audience?" asked James.

"No, for real, I mean. He was shot in the khazi at the Wood Green Empire."

"Tragic," said James.

Harvey nodded. He sat back in his distempered old armchair and unscrewed the top from a half-empty bottle of scotch. In the artificial light of the standard lamp in the corner he could have passed for sixty, instead of his real age, whatever that was.

"Say when," he added, as he started to pour.

The golden coloured liquid was pouring down the sides of his glass onto the tabletop when Boltini finally said 'when'. It was just another exercise in brinkmanship.

"I didn't know you were such a drinker, Jack."

James let it pass. "Only since I started working with you, Harvey. I need something to help me sleep. It's the thought of all those ruined parties, sad, disenchanted kids and their disillusioned parents, wrecked props… failure seems to follow you around. With all your empty promises you should have been a politician."

"Magic's a vocation, Jack, not a job. No one said it would be easy."

"Actually, Harvey, *you* did. That's exactly what you said. I was pulling pints in The Dog and Duck, doing the occasional card trick to pull the birds and then one day, wham! *Blunder Man* arrives on the scene. Six foot two of hot air with dyed blonde hair, looking uncannily like Boris Johnson after a night on the tiles, and telling me how I could earn the easiest hundred quid of my life as your assistant. Join me, James, you said, and your fortune's in the bag. Was that the bag you lost that Cartier watch in last week, or the body bag that poor bloody goldfish died in this afternoon? You're a flaming menace, Harvey."

"Jack, Jack. Wait."

"Harvey, it's over. I don't want to be a laughing stock any longer. I don't want to exist on a diet of beans on toast because I don't know where the next pay cheque is coming from. Here are your car keys," added Boltini, dropping them onto the glass-topped table with a clatter. "I'll get a taxi home if you'll just point me in the right direction for the phone." He didn't actually have the money, but you couldn't make a grand exit by walking off in a fit of pique to catch the bus.

"The phone? Yes, of course. I'm sure it's here somewhere. Try under that pile of laundry," suggested Harvey, vaguely. "Or wait till it rings."

Boltini sat down heavily. "If it only rings when we've got a booking, I could be here till next Christmas," he said.

"It wasn't always like this though, was it?" said Harvey. "Remember the good times? Remember the 2005 Crouch End Police Ball? They loved us. They even tore up your parking ticket."

"*You* tore up my parking ticket," said Boltini, with a smile, "and that damn fool desk sergeant kept waiting for you to magic it back together."

"Touching faith," murmured Harvey. "Now before you go, Jack, I need to tell you something."

"There's nothing you can say I want to hear, Harvey. Tomorrow morning I'm going out to look for a *proper* job."

"That's fine, but I need to confide in someone. You see, *they're* after me and I want to make sure that if they catch up with me, there's someone to notify the Triangle," said Harvey in deadly earnest.

"What's that then," smirked James, "the Cricklewood Knitting Triangle?"

"The Magic Triangle, of course," replied Harvey, gravely.

"I see, Conspiracy Theories R Us now, is it?" said Boltini. "Have you sunk so low?"

"James, please. This is a matter of life or death. You only know me as a not very good magician, right? A buffoon."

"Exactly," concurred Boltini, "I couldn't have put it better myself."

"Well, what if I told you it was all a front and that I'm really a law enforcement agent working in conjunction with the Magic Triangle?" asked Harvey.

"I'd think you were completely bonkers as well as being a crap magician," said Boltini with withering honesty.

"When I got back to the house yesterday, a parcel was waiting for me," continued Harvey, unheeding.

"Yes, and?"

"Inside it was this," said Harvey. He picked up a discarded jiffy bag from the sideboard and emptied the contents onto the floor in front of Boltini.

"Two pieces of broken stick? Wow, I'm frightened."

"Look again, James. They're the two halves of a magician's wand. It's a warning."

"Yeah, but it could be from anyone who's seen your act; anyone who's paid for the dubious privilege anyway."

Harvey sighed wearily. He recharged their glasses then took a sip of whisky.

"Have a drink, James, while I tell you about the Red Square."

"It's in Moscow isn't it?" asked Boltini.

"As I'm sure you know, the Magic Triangle was founded in 1905 at Pinoli's restaurant in London by Derek Deviant, Claude Mastermain and Ying Tong Pong, the famous Chinese magician from St.Louis. But if you think they just set it up for laughs or to have somewhere to go on a Sunday afternoon after the pubs shut, you're sadly mistaken. It wasn't even established to further its members understanding of magic, but to provide an organisation powerful enough to counter the activities of the Red Square. The Square is an ancient order of thieves and vagabonds which came into existence in Rome in the year 1510. Originally it was the creation of Pope Julius the sixteenth, who needed some papers recovering with no questions asked. He commissioned one of his cardinals, Carlo Benedetti, to form a special group of *illusionistas peculiares* which later became known as the Red Square. Each member was a skilled agent; a locksmith, acrobat, soldier, painter and decorator and so on, sworn to absolute secrecy on pain of death and given a thousand ducats to seal his allegiance. There was no task they could not accomplish. Once they'd recovered the pope's missing papers and touched up the Sistine Chapel, they turned their hands to more lucrative pursuits; emptying bank vaults, highway robbery and blackmailing wealthy businessmen.

Too late the pope realised what a monster he'd created and excommunicated them all, hounding them out of civilised society. The outlaws went underground and dispersed across the western world. By 1850 they were active in London, gradually spreading their malign influence throughout the metropolis until, by 1905, the league of English magicians felt compelled to form the Triangle to counter the Square's illegal activities. At first the Triangle met with great success. By 1928 there were thought to be only three members of the Red Square left in the country; Rintizi the dwarf, Giovanni Proscutio and Bram O'Reilly."

"Never heard of them," said Boltini.

"Exactly. They moved like shadows across the land, rarely drawing the attention of the authorities but always being implicated in heinous crimes," continued Harvey.

"So what you're telling me is that the Magic Triangle only exists to fight against an underground organisation of gifted criminals?" asked the slack-jawed Boltini.

"Yes."

"And that this secret society of master criminals is out to get you?"

"Yes," agreed Harvey once more.

"Well, I've never heard such a load of old tosh in my life. How many bottles of whisky did it take to come up with this old pony?"

"I'm sorry you don't want to believe me, but I'm deadly serious," said Harvey.

"So what other messages have you received?" asked Boltini.

"Recently, in fact this afternoon before I left for the show, I came across a dead hedgehog on the path outside."

"Tragic, but what makes you think it has anything to do with the Red Square? Perhaps it just had a walk on part in one of your tricks."

"The hedgehog is one of their mystic symbols."

"You're freakin' mad mate," cried Boltini. "I should get some treatment if I were you." He reflected again on what he had been told and then began looking around the room suspiciously. "Say, you're not winding me up are you, Harvey? You're not filming this conversation for some candid camera show on TV?"

"Boltini, be serious. You have to believe me. Anything is possible if you believe in magic."

"Yeah, I saw what you did to that poor bloody goldfish, mate. Someone ought to set the RSPCA on you."

"Boltini, there's no point in being glib about it, a broken wand can mean only one thing; death is stalking me. If I disappear sometime in the next few days you must go to the Triangle on Stephenson Way and tell the secretary that the Square is on the move. There's more at stake than our careers."

"That's lucky, 'cos mine's shot to hell!" cried Boltini, getting up from his chair and walking to the door. There was only so much bullshit he could take at one sitting.

"You know what they say, Harvey," he concluded as he buttoned up his coat.

"What's that, James, old friend?"

"Don't call us, we'll call you. See you around sometime."

"Goodbye, Boltini."

Part Five

The case is afoot

Sunday morning dawned on Marble Arch. Along the row of benches that stretched from the Arch to the edge of the park, a short well-built gentleman of indeterminate age sat yawning alone. He opened the thermos flask at his side and poured himself a cup of steaming tea. He reached for his lunchbox then thought better of it; not even Hymie Goldman could eat lunch before eight in the morning.

Crowds of Sunday strollers, foreign tourists and gentlemen of the road drifted by like an elaborate tableau of city life. All of them ignored Goldman, as well they might; he had the perfect face for a private investigator - unappealing and entirely forgettable.

Suddenly, from across the park, a man-mountain appeared. With clapped-out red hair and an unfeasibly large overcoat, he bore more than a passing resemblance to a bull mastiff chewing a wasp.

"So, this is where you've been hiding!" said Mike Murphy, as he squatted on the bench next to his elusive business partner, nearly tipping Goldman into a nearby waste bin as the woodwork took the strain.

"You haven't been working on a case after all, have you, Goldman? Just hanging out by the Arch with all the other deadbeats!"

"Mike, give me a break," said Hymie.

"Certainly, which leg?"

"I mean, I *am* on a case. I didn't just come here to eat my sandwiches you know. Anyway, this is hardly the time and place to discuss it."

"What?" persisted Mike.

"My latest investigation," said Hymie, trying to head off further conversation.

"Oh, the racehorse case."

"Redrum," corrected Hymie.

"Shhh… don't give away any confidential information," mocked Mike.

Hymie fished in his coat pocket and removed a wad of fifty pound notes, which he waved in Mike's face.

"I suppose this is a fantasy too!" he cried.

"Blimey, Goldman, you'd better give that to me to hold. You could get mugged for a lot less than that around here. How much is there, anyway? A grand? Two?"

"Try ten, you gormless great lump."

Mike stared at him dumbfounded. "All from the Redrum case?"

"That's just for starters, mate. If I can solve the case, there's a bonus too."

"What's to solve?"

"The whereabouts of a dud magician called *The Amazing Harvey*."

"Any luck so far?" asked Mike.

"No. He hasn't hit the big time yet so his act must be pretty poor."

"With a name like that, is it any wonder?" said Mike. "Where have you looked?"

"Under various stones. So far I've only managed to find where he's been, rather than where he is. He did a couple of diabolical gigs in North Finchley a couple of years ago then disappeared," said Hymie.

"And you suspect foul play?" asked Mike.

"No, it sounds like he was just too ashamed to ever perform in Finchley again. I thought I might try Golders Green or Cricklewood next. I'm looking for the sort of place where lack of ability is no obstacle to getting bookings. Any ideas?"

"Britain's got talent?"

Hymie rolled his eyes. "I thought we might try the Magic Triangle," he said. "If he's a real magician he's sure to be on their books."

"I'd better come along and protect the ten... ahem, *you* from any bother. You know you can rely on me to watch your back," said Mike.

"Yeah, but it's my front I'm worried about," replied Hymie.

They ambled across the road to the nearest taxi rank. Hymie stooped down to the half open window to speak to the cabbie, who was idly flicking through his racing paper at the kerbside.

"Do you know the way to...?"

"San Jose?" ventured the cabbie. "No, but if you hum it, I'll call the police."

"Ho, bloody ho!" said Goldman. "That's all we flamin' need, a cabbie who thinks he's a comedian."

"Where to guv?" asked the suddenly serious cab driver, sensing his fare slipping away. It was his mission in life never to knowingly lose a fare.

"The Magic Triangle," cut in Mike over Hymie's shoulder.

"Gorblimey, you gave me a start. Is this your trained gorilla?" he asked Hymie.

"You talk too much, mate," said Mike, "but I have a solution," he continued, flexing his knuckles ominously.

"Look, we just want to go to the Magic Triangle," said Hymie. "How about it?"

The cabbie appeared to be wracking his brain. "The Magic Triangle? *The* Magic Triangle? The *Magic...*"

"Yeah," said Hymie.

"Where's that then?" he concluded.

"Look, mate, *you're* the cabbie. When I go to a chip shop I don't expect to peel me own spuds. Take us to the flamin' Magic Triangle before I smash yer face in!" snapped Mike.

"Why didn't you say so in the first place," said the cabbie, driving off without them. They had better luck with the taxi behind; not only had the driver heard of the Magic Triangle, but he even knew where

25

to find it and was only too willing to take them there for a modest fee. They shuffled into the back of the cab.

"You know, until a few weeks ago I'd never heard of the Magic Triangle," said the cabbie, "then all of a sudden every loony and nut job in London wants to go there."

Mike began to flex his knuckles again.

"Present company excepted, of course!" added the driver, suddenly catching sight of Mike's grim visage and furrowed brow in his rear view mirror.

"So, what's it all about, H?" asked Mike, as they trundled across the city.

"What's that, Mike?"

"Magic," whispered the big man.

"Ah yes, the old art of deception. Well, some would say it's entertainment in its oldest and purest form, but personally I reckon they're just a bunch of crooks; they take your money and give you nothing in return."

"How long have you been a magician then?" quipped Mike.

"Oh, very funny. Look, mate, we're the good guys around these parts. We sort out people's problems and leave them with a smile on their faces. Where's the deception in that? We provide total commitment, sheer graft and all the legwork needed to get the job done; surely that still has a value in this crazy world?"

Mike shook his head. "I reckon the likes of Ray Decca would disagree with you there, H. We may not be poncing around in flash suits pulling rabbits out of a hat or sawing some dolly bird in half, but as far as he's concerned we're still part of the problem, not the solution. Still, what would life be like without a little magic every now and then?"

Hymie smiled and leant back in the hard plastic seat. Mike may look like a man with no finer feelings but he could surprise you. At times he veered off the straight and narrow into the squashily sentimental.

The taxi pulled up in an empty alley near Euston Station.

"That's the place, there," said the cabbie, pointing at an ominous looking doorway with the number thirteen above the door. "Mum's the word," he added with a wink.

They paid him and shuffled back out of the cab. Once the taxi had gone, they walked the length and breadth of the street to familiarise themselves with the locale.

"Quiet here, innit," said Mike. "It's hard to believe we're in the middle of eight million people."

"That's just what I was thinking," said Hymie. "Yet down this insignificant street it's so quiet that practically anything could happen without anyone knowing."

"Come on, Goldman, let's get on with it," said Mike, pressing the bell.

There was no response.

"What kind of a dive is this anyway, without a bell that works?" said Hymie. "Leave it to me, Mike, I'll soft soap them with the old Goldman charm." He hammered on the door with his fist. "Open up, it's a matter of life or death!" he cried.

There was still no reply. Mike smirked. "So that's what you call charm is it, H? Leave it to me, mate, I do a great line in tact and diplomacy," he added, walking backwards for several metres and preparing to charge at the door. The big man started to run; twenty stone of ex-bouncer moving purposefully at high velocity. As he reached the door its wooden panels receded before him as someone opened the door from within. Mike continued on his trajectory, speeding forwards into the interior before colliding spectacularly with a hat and coat-stand and coming to rest in a heap on the floor.

"Are you alright?" asked the man inside; a smartly dressed youth with a pointy face and horn rimmed spectacles.

"Huuurrrrr, huuurrrrr… never better," said Mike, struggling for breath.

Hymie appeared, as if by magic, in the entrance.

"Can I help you?" asked the representative of the Magic Triangle.

Goldman swept his hand through his hair as though preparing for great oratory, cleared his throat and began.

"My name's Hymie Goldman and this is my business partner, Michael Murphy."

"That's as may be, but we're not open to the public. Do you have an appointment?"

"Ah, yes, I do," lied Hymie. "With Mr..er..." he continued, clutching for some shred of a credible name."

"Gordon Bennett?" suggested the youth with the spectacles.

"Yes, that's it, Gordon Bennett," said Hymie gratefully.

"Well, there's no one here of that name," sneered the youth. "How about Walter Swinburne?"

"Ah, yes...that was it," said Hymie.

"No, never heard of him, he doesn't work here either," said the youth. "You're lying aren't you?"

"Huuuurrr... we're here to see Ali Bongo," said Mike, getting up belatedly from the carpet.

"I'm sorry, you're too late," said the youth.

"Not left already?" said Mike, warming to his work.

"No, he died in 2009."

"Bugger!" said Hymie.

"I'd appreciate it if you would leave now," said the pointy faced youth. Some of us have work to do."

"Look, son," said Hymie, "what's your name?"

"Gerald."

"Look, Gerald, cards on the table. We're a couple of detectives looking for a magician called *The Amazing Harvey*. The sooner you help us out, the sooner we get outta your hair," said Hymie.

"Well, tempting though it is," said Gerald, "I'm just a lowly paid minion in the Magic Triangle, what's in it for me?"

"I'll tell you what's in it for you, you steaming great nit!" cried Mike, pulling himself up to his full height as he lifted Gerald off the ground by the lapels of his suit, ripping one. "You tell us where we can find this guy Harvey, or you'll be spending the next few weeks drinking soup through a straw in the local hospital. Your choice!" he concluded fiercely.

Gerald appeared to be at a loss for words. His mouth was moving but no sound came out.

"Mike, Mike, put him down, for goodness sake," said Hymie. "I know he's an irritating little twerp, but he's hardly a threat, now is he?"

Gerald nodded in enthusiastic support of his saviour.

Mike lowered the shaken pen-pusher to the ground and the colour began to return to Gerald's face.

"So, you see, Gerald, we're reasonable men," said Hymie. "We don't want to hurt you; it's just that we work in a dangerous business, that's all. Sometimes people try to hurt us, but we're men of peace as you can see. I'm sure you'll do your best for us, won't you, Gerald. As I said, all we need is a contact address for *The Amazing Harvey* and then we'll be outta here."

"Believe me, there's nothing I'd rather do than tell you," said Gerald, "but I've never heard of him. Simply practicing magic doesn't qualify you for admittance to the Magic Triangle; we only take the best and brightest. At any time there are simply thousands of semi pro's plying their trade through small ads in newsagents shop windows. If you like I could ask around though. Just leave me your number and I'll call you if I hear anything."

"Do we look stupid?" snapped Mike, lifting Gerald up by the collar again and ripping his other lapel. "We give you our number and the next thing we know is the cops are on our doorstep giving us the third degree for roughing you up in the Magic Triangle. We weren't born yesterday, you little jerk!"

"Mike, Mike…it's not worth it. Put him down," said Hymie.

Mike lowered the crumpled remains of Gerald to the floor. He promptly made a run for it.

"Thank you very much, you great nurk!" said Hymie. "That's why you should let me do the talking. We're supposed to be a couple of streetwise detectives solving cases with our wits and cunning, not a couple of mindless thugs scaring the crap out of unsuspecting members of the public who just happen to be in the wrong place at the wrong time. Gerald could have become a valued contact in this illustrious organisation instead of a new member of the 'We Hate JP Confidential Society'."

Mike hung his head dejectedly and shuffled his feet.

"Anyway, we'd better get out of here before security arrives," added Hymie.

They beat a hasty retreat for the exit. As Hymie stepped out onto the pavement, a revving engine sounded out from somewhere nearby and a red sports car raced down the street towards him. It hurtled along the road, mounted the pavement outside the doorway to number thirteen and sped on towards the startled sleuth.

CRUNCH!

Hymie reeled backwards into a world of silence and darkness. All Mike could see as he gazed down the street after the disappearing sports car was the back of a woman's head. She may have had dark curly hair and been wearing a red jacket and scarf, but he couldn't be sure.

Part Six

All unquiet on the Cricklewood Front

There are parts of Cricklewood which are practically no go zones for the working classes, assuming such people still exist. Streets where the Union Jack still flies over the manicured lawns of old Blighty and where Darjeeling and cucumber sandwiches are still *de rigeur* at four o'clock. It was into such a street that Inspector Decca and his chauffeur, Sergeant Terse, were decanted one sunny afternoon; two extraterrestrials on parole from Planet Portaloo.

For Decca, as welcome as it was to extricate himself from the bowels of Police HQ, a sense of foreboding had begun to trouble him; a feeling that it was all very well associating with the rich and powerful until it all went pear shaped and he was left carrying the can. Terse, blithely unaware of such possibilities, lived in a less rarefied world; a world in which a crook in a big house was still a crook, he just got away with it more often. He little cared for subtlety or sophistication, all that mattered was that he was *the law*. He would have felt right at home in Dodge City, but if it had to be Cricklewood, so be it.

They slammed the doors of the patrol car they'd commandeered and crunched their way down the gravel path to the imposing front door, inlaid with elaborate stained glass panels, no doubt nicked from the local church, thought Terse.

"OK, Terse, don't say *anything*," said Decca. "If you have to speak at all, try and stick to the weather or Andy Murray's chances at Wimbledon. On second thoughts, forget the tennis." Sergeant Terse reached out a sausage-like finger and pressed the doorbell three times in quick succession.

"Alright, sir," said Terse, who really wanted to shout 'Open Up! It's the Fuzz!'.

The door opened to reveal a mature and smartly dressed lady of a certain age, whose face, as she saw the police car, shifted down a gear from polite indifference to irked dismay.

"Don't you people drive *ordinary* cars nowadays?" she asked, with massive condescension.

Decca flashed his credentials. "Inspector Decca, CID," he said, curtly. "This is my colleague, Sergeant Terse. And you would be?"

"Mrs Olga Flanagan, of course, who else would I be?"

Decca raised an eyebrow. Terse determinedly said nothing.

"Can we come in, or would you rather discuss matters on the doorstep?" asked Decca.

"No, please come in," said their reluctant hostess. "I take it you've come about the so-called magician?"

He nodded and they followed her through the house into a large and airy conservatory at the rear of the property.

"It was down there that it happened," said Mrs Flanagan, pointing out of the window towards the end of the garden.

"I see," said Decca. "I've read the statement you made, of course, but it helps to see where the alleged incident occurred."

"There's nothing *alleged* about it," snapped Mrs Flanagan. "It was a despicable act by a depraved madman masquerading as a children's entertainer."

Decca coughed to suppress a smirk. "Yes, of course," he said. "It must have been very distressing for you and the children. I hope you're feeling a bit better now."

"Well hardly," continued the lady of the house. "Poor little Sophie may never be the same again, not to mention Sammy, who was practically one of the family."

"Sammy?" queried Terse, flipping through his notebook, pencil in hand.

"Sammy the goldfish, of course!" exclaimed Olga Flanagan. "Why, when I think of his sweet little face pressed up against the glass when we had visitors it makes me so sad. Sad and angry that that *monster* could ..." she continued.

"Ah, so Sammy's the squashed goldfish," said Terse. "I see, now we're getting somewhere. Do you still have the body, madam?" he continued, forgetting Decca's recent instruction to be quiet at all costs.

Mrs Flanagan's eyes boggled. She couldn't believe what she was hearing. "No," she said.

"You see, madam," continued Terse, while Decca gaped like a goldfish out of water, "we need evidence; hard facts and reliable testimony from upright, respectable citizens like yourself. Kids just don't cut it in the courts. If you want us to put this sleazebag behind bars where he belongs, you'll have to show us a bit more than an empty bowl and a business card for *The Amazing Harvey – magic like you wouldn't believe*," he said, reading from the card. "I mean, come on, lady, by your own admission you didn't pay him so what are we looking at here? Criminal damage to a missing fish? He'll probably get off with a caution. He may even sue."

"Wu, wu, wu...yu..." was all the apoplectic Mrs Flanagan could manage.

Decca seized the opportunity to regain control of the interview.

"That'll be enough, thank you, Terse," he said. "Mrs Flanagan, please excuse my colleague. He's a very good officer but he's a little too used to dealing with hardened criminals. Clearly his sense of discretion has become a casualty of our difficult work."

He proffered a large white handkerchief.

Mrs Flanagan took it and blew her nose into it. "I do understand, Inspector," she said, with some effort. "Junior staff should speak when they're spoken to," she added, arching an eyebrow at the oblivious Terse.

"Nevertheless," continued Decca, "there's much truth in what the sergeant says."

Olga Flanagan drew herself up to her full five feet three inches. "That's simply not good enough, Inspector. This man, Harvey, is a menace to law abiding citizens everywhere and I fully intend to have him struck off as a children's entertainer. He should be exposed to the full force of the law. My daughter and the other children at her party may be emotionally scarred for life! Steps must be taken and they must be taken now. If you don't take them, then I will, and as I'm sure you know I have friends in some very high places."

Terse, who had friends in some very low places, stared out of the window.

Inspector Decca stood his ground. "I trust, madam, you're not suggesting that the law can be manipulated to serve the interests of a chosen few. I can assure you that the Metropolitan Police take these matters very seriously and we will be taking all the steps necessary to bring this perpetrator to justice. Although, in my experience, this kind of lowlife never sticks around anywhere long enough to suffer the consequences of his crimes."

"Have you thought about hiring a private detective?" asked Terse, impulsively.

"That'll do, thank you, Terse. Be quiet!" snapped Decca.

"No, Inspector, let the man speak," said Mrs Flanagan. "It's the first sensible thing he's said since he arrived."

Terse smiled fatuously. He'd been in this woman's company for less than twenty minutes and although he was no rocket scientist, he could already tell that she was a time-wasting, whinging old battleaxe with no conception of life outside the NW2 postcode. If he could palm her off on Hymie Goldman, he may just be able to avoid running around like a headless chicken on a pointless investigation for two months before being demoted to an even smaller office.

"You were saying, Terse?" prompted the Inspector, scarcely believing he was actually going along with this madness.

"We can't compete with private detectives on cases like this," began Terse. Decca closed his eyes.

"Our hands are tied," continued Terse. "You need someone who can give your case all the time and attention it needs, fight fire with fire, get their hands dirty. As policemen we have to abide by the law, we have to respect the human rights of scum like this, who really need a good kicking. Personally, I'd like to punch this guy's face in, but can I? Not ruddy likely, I'd be on the dole before you could say Jack Robinson."

"I like the cut of your jib, Sergeant," said Olga Flanagan at the thought of *The Amazing Harvey* having his face rearranged. "Can you recommend anyone?"

Decca quickly re-opened his eyes. This couldn't be happening; even Terse had more sense than that, surely?

"Officially, no. But off the record, madam, there *is* a man I've come across in the course of my duties who may fit the bill," said Terse. "He seems to have a way of inflicting a kind of natural justice on those he meets without any conscious effort. He's also cheap; you can usually beat him down to practically nothing."

"Excellent, Sergeant, and his name is?"

"Hymie Goldman. He works out of an office on the Finchley Road, above the Black Kat café. The business is called J P Confidential. No case is too small, nothing too much trouble. Mention my name if you like. Tell him I recommended him," said Terse, grinning.

"Thank you, Sergeant, you've been most helpful," said Mrs Flanagan. Sammy must be avenged! she thought.

We're all going to hell! thought Decca.

If we can get going in the next five minutes I may just get back in time for the match, thought Terse, as the two policemen retraced their steps to their patrol car.

Part Seven

There's no people like show people

In a threadbare old theatre in north London, Marvin the Marvellous Mechanical prepared for his umpteenth comeback tour with barely concealed indifference. He was a dapper little man in his late fifties, immaculately dressed in faultless evening wear and carrying a top hat, but he seemed listless as he went through his stage preparations.

"Five minutes to curtain up!" cried a voice backstage.

Marvin straightened out the props on his conjuring table and checked his pockets for the key to his once famous *Cabinet of Doom*, a rusting metal hulk, now painted lime green and concealed from view at the back of the stage. Boy, he'd played some dives in his time but this place took the biscuit. The masonry was crumbling, the lights flickered and the audience looked like they'd escaped from a day-care centre. In fact, they were simply sheltering from the downpour outside until the number 28 bus arrived.

Marvin wondered briefly how places like this could pay the rent, then caught sight of the posters for recent attractions, reflected on the pittance they were paying him and remembered. Ah, yes, *Harry Bosworth and Mr Jinks,* a dire ventriloquist act from Pinner which relied too heavily on the audience's ability to imagine it was being entertained. As for *The Peckham Pirouettes*, the critic, Roy Santiago, of *Then and Now* magazine had described them as 'a bunch of fat, bored, middle-aged women with no skill or training, sucking the life-blood out of local entertainment'. How he'd laughed when they caught up with him outside the newsagents on the High Street a few days later. You didn't hear so much of Roy these days; probably still in hospital.

The moth-eaten satin curtain sailed slowly away into the slips, leaving Marvin to his fate. As the scant crowd sat dripping in the aisles, suppressing a collective yawn of anticipation, he strode purposefully to the front of the stage to address them.

"Ladies and gentlemen, how do?"

Nothing. Not a ripple. Not a flicker. Scarcely a neuron connected among the lot of them.

"I'm Marvin the Marvellous Mechanical and I have an amazing magic show for you tonight to rival anything in the world. This act has been performed before the crowned heads of Europe. They hated it, that's why I'm presenting it to you tonight in this burnt out public lavatory. Only kidding," he added as an afterthought.

"Before I begin the act for which I am rightly famous, let me introduce my assistant this evening; the lovely, the unscrew…sorry, inscrutable, Miss Lotus Blossom." A short, blousy, middle-aged woman, flimsily disguised as a geisha girl in a cropped black wig, shuffled onto the stage, bowed and shuffled off again. Her real name was Doris Biggs.

"Thank you, thank you, Miss Lotus Blossom," said Marvin.

There was a half-hearted ripple of applause. A couple of people left.

He smiled then opened his mouth to reveal what appeared to be an egg. He carefully removed it and flattened it on the top of his hat. A cloud of white smoke appeared above him and a pigeon seemed to fly out of the top of the hat before fluttering down to the back of the stage, where it left a deposit on Lotus Blossom's wig.

The theatre was silent. You could have heard a pin drop, had the floor not been covered in chewing gum and empty sweet wrappers.

Unappreciative bastards, thought Marvin.

"I dare say you've seen stage magic before, that you think it's all sleight of hand and trickery," he said, "but tonight, ladies and gentlemen, I'm going to give you a performance you will never forget; a show of such power and ingenuity you may be excused for thinking me the devil incarnate."

The slow drift to the bus stop continued.

"Lotus Blossom, please to assist me," said the Marvellous Mechanical to his assistant, with a bow. The ageing geisha tiptoed across the stage and handed him what looked like a large red house brick.

He took it and held it out for the audience to see. "One common or garden house brick," he said.

"How do we know it's real?" asked a man in the third row of the stalls.

Marvin simply let go of the brick and watched it land on the stage with a crunch.

A young girl at the back of the theatre began to laugh hysterically but anyone looking around soon noticed that the right-hand side of her face was illuminated, presumably by her mobile phone.

Marvin stooped down to retrieve the brick, kicking away the traces of red dust.

"I think we've established that we're dealing with a real brick here," said Marvin, "but not everything is as it seems," he added. "If I were to tell you I could transform this simple brick into something entirely different by the sheer power of magic, what would you wish for, ladies and gentlemen?"

"A coupl'a hot biatches and some coke, man," called out a shady character at the rear of the stalls.

"Thank you, Chief Constable, but I'm afraid I'm only a magician, not a politician. Anyone else?" asked Marvin, scouring the auditorium for a sympathetic face.

"Well, I've been trying to get my hands on a Ford Cortina Mark 3 distributor cap for ages," said a balding middle-aged man with his arms folded across his chest.

Marvin retrieved a large white handkerchief from his top pocket and blew his nose despondently. After all these years he never failed to be disappointed by his fellow man's complete lack of imagination. They simply had no sense of wonder.

"I'm sure you have, mate, but have you tried eBay?" said Marvin, dismissively. "Would anyone else care to wish for something?"

"A lovely big bunch of flowers," said a sweet little old lady in an aisle seat.

"A wonderful idea, my dear lady, and I shall be only too happy to oblige," said Marvin with relief. After all, how the hell was he meant to fit a Mark 3 distributor cap up his sleeve?

"Abracadabra, super glue, roses are red and violets, blue!" exclaimed Marvin, dramatically.

Someone began to titter at the absurdity of it all.

"What goes up must come down," said Marvin, throwing the brick up into the air.

There was a loud popping sound and the brick vanished in a puff of white smoke, to be replaced by a cascade of paper daisies, which showered the stage in a blanket of coloured petals.

Marvin took his first bow and was gratified to hear the audience applaud warmly.

"Thank you, my friends," he murmured.

Lotus Blossom tiptoed back across the stage, tapped her wristwatch and whispered something into Marvin's ear.

"Ladies and gentlemen, now for the pièce de résistance of this evening's performance, the moment you've all been waiting for; the *Cabinet of Doom*, featuring the *Pendulum of Death,*" said Marvin. He nodded to Lotus Blossom to wheel the great hulking contraption to the front of the stage as he continued his patter.

"I'm sure you've all heard of the famous Harry Houdini, well the illusion I am about to present to you would have baffled even the great escapologist himself." He carefully removed his jacket and hat and placed them neatly on the floor. He stretched out his arms and turned full circle on the stage before the audience to demonstrate he had nothing to hide.

"In a moment, ladies and gentlemen, I will be secured by official police-issue handcuffs inside the small compartment on the left-hand side of the *Cabinet of Doom*. Inside the cabinet itself..." he paused for effect and for Lotus Blossom to open the front of the lime green metal box, "is the *Pendulum of Death;* a razor sharp blade swinging back and forth inside the case. It is restrained from swinging for an absolute maximum of three minutes by these special retaining cords," he said, pointing to what looked like a couple of old mooring ropes. "If I fail to extricate myself from the handcuffs within three minutes and exit through the door at the back of the cabinet, the pendulum's blade will first slice through the restraining ropes and then through myself." He gazed intently into the auditorium.

The last few remaining audience members fell into a hushed silence.

Marvin covered his eyes with a blindfold and was escorted into place by his assistant, Lotus Blossom. She carefully attached the handcuffs to his wrists and left the chamber, closing the metal door firmly behind her. Finally she pressed the starter button on an outsized stopwatch mounted on a stand at the front of the stage and a drum roll sounded out across the theatre's ancient PA system.

As the seconds ticked by on the stopwatch, an increasing air of tension and anticipation gripped the remaining seven members of the audience. The atmosphere was electric. With thirty seconds to go there was a loud banging sound from inside the chamber, as though someone were desperately trying to escape. There was still no sign of Marvin. Twenty five seconds came and went, twenty, fifteen, the excitement was palpable. Lotus Blossom began to look more concerned than inscrutable. Ten seconds remaining, then five, then three, two and one passed and the audience gave an audible sigh as the sound of the pendulum swinging inside the cabinet grew louder. A trickle of dark liquid pooled onto the stage from the left side of the cabinet. Lotus Blossom ran to the wings and shouted for help. The safety curtain came down and the show ended abruptly.

As the last member of the audience stumbled out onto the street, stunned and fearful that he had witnessed the death of Marvin the Marvellous Mechanical, Lotus Blossom opened the door of the *Cabinet of Doom,* barely able to look.

Inside, everything was in a state of utter confusion. The pendulum had sheared through the retaining ropes and battered the sides of the cabinet, which were now protruding beyond their normal position. The trail of liquid which had trickled onto the stage appeared to originate from the pendulum's hydraulic system. The escape door at the back of the cabinet was wide open but there was no sign of Marvin, except for a pair of artificial arms hanging absurdly from the unopened handcuffs.

Down the corridor behind the stage, Marvin walked past the empty dressing rooms towards the stage door. That bloody useless machine, he knew he should have had it serviced properly. It was just as well he'd been using those artificial arms or he'd be a gonner by now. He pushed open the stage door and walked out into the darkened street. Suddenly there was a noise from overhead. He turned and looked up. The last thing he saw was a red house brick approaching his head at high speed.

Part Eight

A day in the life of Hymie Goldman

Goldman awoke to find himself in a strange bed with a severe headache. It wasn't even symptomatic of a wild and hectic social life, as he was well and truly alone. Where exactly was he? What had he been doing the night before and what day was this? he wondered briefly. He should have known better at his age. Ah well, he'd just have to pop out for some headache tablets from that new mega-chemist by the ring road, Hyper-Chondria.

The shapely rear of a woman in white overalls hove into view as she pulled open the blinds with a flourish. Aaarrghh! That was one sight he could do without, daylight! He'd never been a morning person.

"Nurse, please close the blinds, I'm not big on sunshine this early in the day," said Hymie.

"Oh, sorry," said the girl, partly closing them. "Although it's gone eleven and I'm not a nurse. My name's Ruby. Mike asked me if I could do a bit of cleaning, cash in hand." She looked at him curiously for a moment. She was a coloured girl of about thirty with playful brown eyes and a dazzling smile.

"I see," said Hymie. "So, where are we?"

"Don't you recognise your own office?" asked Ruby, laughing.

"Frankly, no. You're not trying to tell me this is 792A Finchley Road, surely?"

"Oh, but I am," said Ruby.

"I don't believe it. It's never looked like this in my time here. Where did this bed come from?" asked Hymie.

"Well, I must admit the place was in a real state when I got here. You wouldn't have believed the dust."

"There goes our filing system," said Hymie, petulantly.

"As for the bed, it's just a convertible sofa that Mike moved in from the reception area."

Hymie smiled. "Well, thank you, Ruby, you've done a great job," he said. "Mike has some marvellous friends I never knew about."

He blushed slightly, despite his best efforts not to. He wasn't used to dealing with attractive cleaning ladies, only women who hated his guts or were trying to con him. "Would you be interested in a full time job?" he asked, as casually as he could manage.

"What, as a cleaner?" asked Ruby.

"Well, as you can probably tell, we're only a small business, we can't afford to pay a full time cleaner but if you can do office admin, answer the phone and make a decent cuppa too, the job's yours. If it works out you could even train as a private investigator one day." replied Hymie.

"I don't know about that but office manager's a good place to start. How much are you paying?" she asked.

He looked into her big brown eyes and forgot entirely what he was about to say.

"Err…what are you earning now?" asked Hymie.

"£18K plus overtime," she replied.

He realised too late he was in too deep but couldn't bear to admit it to himself.

"Well, I'm sure we could manage an extra 5%," he said.

Ruby looked around the room dubiously. They couldn't afford to pay her nearly £19K a year. She'd be surprised if they took home that much themselves, but then she was between jobs and she hadn't earned £18K in the first place.

"It's a deal," she said. "When do I start, Mr Goldman?"

"Welcome on board, Ruby," said Hymie, "and it's *Hymie*. Nobody calls me *Mr Goldman* except the bailiffs and HM Revenue and Customs, and they always manage to make it sound like an insult."

The phone rang in reception. Hymie winced.

"No peace for the wicked," he said. "Why don't you make us both a cup of tea while I answer that," he added, reaching for the phone.

"Hello, Mrs Flanagan..."

"No, this is JP Confidential, you've got the wrong number, love," he said, dropping the receiver.

The phone rang again almost immediately. Blimey! Two calls in one afternoon and they said there was a recession on, he thought.

"Hello, JP Confidential, no case too large," said Hymie.

"*This* is Mrs Flanagan. I'd like to speak to the manager please. I was just cut off by some idiot."

"Speaking... I mean I'm the manager, the proprietor in fact. Goldman's the name, Hymie Goldman, how can I help you, madam?"

"You were recommended to me by a policeman," she said.

Hymie's face fell. It damn near abseiled off a cliff. He tried to avoid the Fuzz wherever possible so the thought of actually being recommended by one of them made his blood run cold.

"Anyone I might know?" he asked.

"Yes, Sergeant someone or other, Tense I think. Yes, Sergeant Tense," continued Mrs Flanagan.

Hymie grimaced. Tense was an apt description of anyone having dealings with Sergeant Terse.

"I think you mean Terse, madam," he said.

"Well, he *was* a little abrupt and to the point, but a good man all the same. He had very enlightened views on the punishment of offenders."

Hymie's mind boggled.

"What sort of case is it?" he asked.

"I want you to find someone and put the fear of God in him."

It sounds like a case for Terse, thought Hymie. "And you're sure the sergeant recommended *me*?" he asked.

"He said it was right up your street," continued Olga Flanagan. "I think he'd have liked to handle the case himself but his inspector said that their resources were a little stretched."

Hymie could imagine Decca saying it, yet why would they recommend *him* when they both thought he was a complete plonker? It all seemed a bit fishy. Still, as long as she was good for the money did it really matter? He'd long since given up expecting anything in his life to make sense.

"He seemed to rate you very highly, Mr Goldman," continued Mrs Flanagan, "he even said your charges were reasonable."

"How kind of him," said Hymie testily. Either Terse was having a laugh or marking his card not to overcharge the old dear on pain of a social call. Or maybe she was just trying it on, you could never be sure. "Perhaps you'd like to arrange an appointment to come in and discuss the details?" he suggested.

"Is that strictly necessary, Mr Goldman? I simply want you to find a deranged madman called *The Amazing Harvey* who masquerades as a magician and children's entertainer and persuade him to retire immediately or else…"

"Or else what exactly?" asked Hymie.

"I'll leave it to your discretion," said Mrs Flanagan.

Hymie fell silent. He couldn't believe his ears. He'd spent years totally oblivious to the existence of *The Amazing Harvey* and then suddenly everyone he met was offering him money to find the guy. If only he knew where he was.

"I could pop you a cheque in the post," added Mrs Flanagan.

It just got better and better. Hymie was on the point of pinching himself when Ruby returned with a mug of steaming tea to find him grinning broadly. She placed the mug on the desk in front of him, passed him a scribbled note then waved and left.

"Damn!" said Goldman. She hasn't resigned already? he thought.

"I beg your pardon, Mr Goldman, there's no need for that," said Mrs Flanagan.

"Sorry, Mrs Flannel…"

"Flanagan!"

"…my assistant just spilt a hot drink over my trousers," said Hymie hastily, as he tried to read the note which was upside down on his desk. It looked like 'need to arrange cat litter, see you tomorrow, R.'

"Did you say you wanted me to find *The Amazing Harvey*? The magician?" he asked. He'd always thought it must be impossible to get paid twice for solving the same case. Getting paid once was hard enough but this seemed to open up all kinds of possibilities.

There was a snort of disgust from the other end of the phone. "Magician? Hah! That's what he calls himself," said Mrs Flanagan, with considerable hauteur. "Bet he couldn't magic himself out of a paper bag. Do I take it you've heard of him, Mr Goldman?"

"No," said Hymie quickly, "but I think I can find him for you."

"Excellent," said Olga Flanagan.

"I normally charge £250 per day plus expenses but as you're a friend of Sergeant Terse, I'll do it for a flat fee of £1,000. Just send a cheque to JP Confidential, 792A Finchley Road, with your contact details and anything you can remember about Harvey and I'll get cracking."

"Well, it's a lot of money, Mr Goldman, but under the circumstances, you have a deal."

"Thanks for the call, Mrs Flanagan, and rest assured I'll do a good job for you," said Hymie, replacing the receiver.

"Yeehah! We're in the money…" he sang tunelessly to himself in the empty office. So what if the neighbours thought he was barmy? For once everything seemed to be coming up trumps. Even his headache had disappeared.

Mike arrived and looked pensively at his dishevelled business partner.

"I suppose you know I saved your life again, Goldman," he said.

"How so, you great lug?" queried Hymie.

"Don't you remember the sports car that nearly flattened you outside the Magic Triangle?"

"No," said Hymie. "I don't believe it. What are you after, Mike?"

"Typical! That's all the thanks I get. I yanked you out of the way at the last minute, Goldman, but because you can't remember it, it never happened. Next time I won't bother, you ungrateful git. I expect you lost your memory when you hit your head on the doors. Still, no harm done eh? No sense, no feeling," added Mike.

"If you say so, Mike. By the way, I've hired a new receptionist cum bottle-washer."

"What are you paying her in? Green Shield stamps?" asked Mike.

"Don't you start, it's that bird Ruby you sent round to do a bit of cleaning. I thought she was a friend of yours," said Hymie.

"Well, not exactly." said Mike. "I advertised for a cleaner for my flat and she was the only one who gave me a quote after she saw the place. The others ran screaming from the building or said they'd suddenly decided to give up the cleaning business for health reasons."

"Well, that's a sort of reference," said Hymie, a wistful look flitting across his face.

"You fancy her, don't you?" asked Mike.

"Don't be ridiculous," said Hymie, avoiding the question. "Besides, someone else has just offered to pay us to find *The Amazing Harvey.*"

"Now that *is* amazing," said Mike. "Who?"

"Some woman called Flanagan. She said Terse recommended us."

"Now we're in trouble," said Mike. "I thought we'd be in clover with this case but if this guy Harvey is of interest to the likes of Terse and Decca, we'd better keep our wits about us."

"Never fear, Mike, we're a match for the whole lot of 'em," said Hymie.

Part Nine

In the Big Room

Inspector Decca walked resignedly along the tenth floor corridor and knocked at the Chief's door on the end at the left, next to the fire escape. The Chief was too important to fry if the office burnt down, thought Decca.

"Come in, Decca," said the wood-alcohol voice, seemingly through three feet of cotton wool.

The Inspector entered the room, approached the Chief's desk and awaited further instructions. He cast a glance at the collection of framed photos around the walls; the Chief being presented with a long service medal, the Chief winning his local golf club annual umbrella, the Chief outside Buckingham Palace en route to a garden party; the Chief pissed out of his mind at some dinner for civic dignitaries, the Chief having a punch-up with Rod Hull and Emu.

"Sit down, Decca," said the Chief.

He sat, still wondering whether he was there for a kick up the arse or a pat on the back. He could swing for that idiot, Terse; nothing any good ever came of recommending Hymie Goldman as a private detective. It was so self evident as to be blindingly obvious to everyone, it seemed, but Terse.

"Well, Decca!" barked the Chief, a tall, heavily built man in his late fifties with a blotchy red face and bright blue eyes. He directed his keen gaze at Decca like a search-light trying to spot an escaped convict.

"What have you been up to eh?"

"Well, sir…" said Decca. He wondered if he should blame it all on Terse, whatever it was, but realised it wouldn't do any good and simply smiled sheepishly.

"Bloody good job, Decca. Excellent work," blurted his commanding officer.

"Thank you, sir," said Decca, perplexed.

"I don't know how you did it, man, and I don't *want* to know but well done. I've been expecting to get it in the neck from Lord O'Connor over his granddaughter's goldfish for days but not only has this not happened but I've actually had a call from the old boy congratulating me on your enlightened policing methods," said the Chief.

Decca could tell it had come as something of a surprise by the way the Chief kept scratching his head.

"Well, of course, sir, I have my methods," said the Inspector.

"I'm sure you do, Ray, and I'm sorry we haven't always seen eye to eye on everything. When you went barmy I had no choice other than to transfer you off the front line, but now I can see you're ready for a bigger challenge. You're a top man, Decca and you've been languishing in a pokey little office with dead flies…I mean files, for far too long. I want you back in Homicide tomorrow, Ray, and I always get what I want. To show that there's no hard feelings you can even take that loony sergeant with you. What's his name again?"

"Terse, sir,"

"Well, whatever. I'm sure we can just go back to losing the paperwork for those unsolved cases down the radiator like we used to." They had to cut costs somehow.

"Yes, sir, very kind of you, sir," said Decca. It was easier to put up with Terse than explain to the Chief that the man was a complete nightmare to work with.

"When you get back to Homicide, Decca there's a case I'd like you to investigate," continued the Chief. "One of those magician fellers turned up outside a theatre with his head bashed in; nasty business. Still, magicians are a damn funny lot; ripping up playing cards and hiding rabbits for a living, very strange."

"Yes, sir," said the Inspector.

"OK, good job, Decca, now get lost."

Ray Decca stood up and walked to the door. There was a spring in his step once more, as he retraced his steps back down the corridor to the lift. Was his luck finally turning for the better? Was he about to join the greats of his profession at last? Only the realisation that he was still lumbered with Terse and Goldman put a dampener on things. Yet perhaps he could even do something about that.

Part Ten

The mystery deepens

Hymie Goldman sat picking his nose behind his desk at 792A Finchley Road. That was the beauty of having no staff, he reflected, you didn't have to bother with the niceties of office life. He scratched his unshaven chin and retrieved a half-eaten bowl of cornflakes from the drawer in his desk. He couldn't remember leaving them there but he supposed he must have done. The intercom buzzer sounded downstairs and he leant across his desk to answer it.

"Who is it?" he asked.

"Ruby, Mr Goldman, your new PA. I said I'd be here as soon as I'd sorted out a cat sitter."

A dreamy look passed across the scruffy detective's face as he recalled their meeting of the day before.

"Come in," he cooed, pressing the door release button.

She seemed to float into the room, a vision in a tight-fitting blouse and pencil skirt. His mouth opened involuntarily but nothing came out apart from a part-chewed cornflake. He brushed it away hastily and smiled.

"Where shall I start then, Hymie?" she asked.

"How about making us both a cuppa?" he said. "I'm sorry I'm in such a state, love, I lost track of the time. I'll go and have a shave and a wash and then we can get started."

As Hymie shuffled off to break the habits of a lifetime, Mike arrived.

"Hello, Ruby. Hymie told me you were joining us. I hope you know what you're letting yourself in for, he's a bit disorganised, to say the least."

"Oh, hi, Mike. Don't worry. He's paying me well. Besides, I've seen your flat, remember?"

Mike grimaced. "Okay, pot, kettle, black, sure," he said, but he still couldn't fathom why Goldman was splashing out cash they could ill afford on this girl. Was Mike - the Mug - Murphy now subsidising the old fool's love life? After all, this was the guy who wouldn't even shell out for a packet of chocolate hobnobs for a partners' meeting. Still, you couldn't say that to the new office junior, reflected Mike.

Goldman returned from his ablutions, clean shaven and wearing a tie. Mike did a double-take.

"Can I help you, sir?" he asked.

Hymie frowned. "It wouldn't hurt you to smarten yourself up for once either, Murphy," he said.

In the time it had taken for Hymie to transform himself, Mike had put away the fold-up bed and Ruby had prepared the drinks.

Hymie beamed at them both with something akin to enthusiasm.

"Team," he began, "I've felt for some time now that we needed to put JP Confidential on the map. Of course, this takes time but every great journey starts with one small step; in our case, holding formal team meetings where we can pool our knowledge, hone our plans and get a real sense of team spirit going."

Mike stared blankly at his senior partner. It was news to him that Goldman ever thought about the business at all, let alone as anything other than his personal cash point.

"Otherwise," continued Hymie, "it's just me and him," he said, nodding at Mike, "sitting around trying to score points off each other."

"Completely pointless, you mean," said Mike.

"Exactly," concurred Hymie. "So if you'd care to pop out and get us some proper cakes," he said to Ruby, proffering a twenty pound note, "then we can start as we mean to go on."

Once she'd left them, Mike leant against the wall and looked out through the blinds onto the street below. A smartly dressed Polish girl called Zuszka was mopping vomit off the pavement outside the Black Kat before any of their customers could tread it into the café.

"That Zuszka's a bit of alright, eh, H? She can use a mop too. That's what I've been missing," said Mike.

"A mop?" queried Hymie.

"No, you plonker! A bit of female company. Don't you ever miss it?"

"What, the abject poverty, the barely concealed hostility and the brooding silence of mutual loathing? I get enough of that here," said Hymie, sarcastically.

"So you're not interested in Ruby, then? It wouldn't bother you if I asked her out sometime?" asked Mike.

"I thought you fancied that Polish bird."

"I see," said Mike.

"See what?" asked Hymie.

"Oh, nothing," said Mike. "Just that we'd better start focusing on the case. We need results and we need them now, before this Redrum guy comes looking for his money back. How hard can it be to find a bum magician called *The Amazing Harvey*?"

"Surprisingly so," said Hymie. "If he was any good he'd have his name plastered everywhere, but as he's rotten, he seems to be virtually untraceable. Still, we haven't exhausted all the possible leads yet. What if I get Ruby to go to the library and check all the local papers for the last few years?"

"Have you already checked him out on the internet, then?" asked Mike.

"Yeah, well, I'm pretty good at investigations you can do from your own armchair."

"You can say that again," said Mike.

Hymie smiled but resisted the temptation.

"So, tell me something more about the client, H. I know he's paid you a pile of cash, but what else do you know about this guy, Redrum?" asked Mike.

"There's not much to tell, Mike, except the guy is seriously weird; a whole other level of odd. He just showed up out of nowhere, like some kind of ghost."

"When was he here?" asked Mike.

"Oh, he's never set foot in the office," continued Hymie.

"Well, I keep telling you we need better offices," said Mike.

"And offices cost money," said Hymie emphatically. "Anyway, I met him a couple of weeks ago on a Tuesday. I remember 'cause I'd been to the flicks to see a late night showing of *The Killers* at the Freemont. I was standing in the doorway downstairs, trying to find my keys without making too much noise, when this shadow fell across me and scared the crap out of me. I turned round and there was this tall guy wearing a black cape."

"Like Batman," interjected Mike.

"Yeah, that sort of thing," said Hymie.

"What did he look like?" asked Mike, feeling strangely sleepy as he sat back in his chair.

"I couldn't really say," said Hymie. "I've never seen his face. He may not even have one, for all I know. You see he stood between me and the beam from the streetlamp. All I saw was his silhouetted shape behind the cape. Then, in a creepy Eastern European accent, he started telling me how he wanted me to find some magician called *The Amazing Harvey*. My first thought was that he must be an escaped madman and that I'd better humour him in case he pulled a gun on me, so I nodded a good deal and said yes at the right moments, and at the end he gave me a case full of money and said he'd be in touch."

"Great. We've got another homicidal maniac for a client," said Mike, suppressing a yawn. "By the way, what's that buzzing noise outside and why are the lights flickering, H?"

"S'funny, I was wondering the same thing, Mi..." said Hymie, leaning back in his chair.

"Zzzzzzzz," said Mike.

"Zzzzzzzz," concurred Hymie.

Some hours later, Goldman was awoken by a wet rasping sensation on his forehead. His eyes flickered open. Everything was dark and he seemed to be alone in the office. Outside, the noise of the traffic suggested it was late in the evening.

Another wet rasping sensation tickled his face.

"Purrrrrrrrrr."

"Bloody hell, Bacon, thanks a bundle!" snapped Hymie, pushing the cat to one side.

Bacon was a street cat Mike had befriended in a moment of weakness. He occasionally sneaked into the office when no one was watching and nicked any left-overs he found lying around. He'd earned his name after Hymie had caught him stealing his breakfast roll.

"Get the hell out of my office, you freeloading fleabag!" snapped Hymie, as he stood up to switch on the lights. He drew the blinds and sat down again. What the blazes was going on? He looked at his watch, which, if it could be believed, was showing 11pm. What had happened to Mike? And Ruby? How long did it take to buy a few cakes? It looked like he could kiss that twenty quid goodbye. Yet something inside kept telling him that it was worse than that; that Mike would never leave without saying goodbye or waking him up. So what had happened to him?

Bacon had retreated to Hymie's desk, where he sat licking himself conscientiously from tail to toe.

"Why didn't you do something, you useless feline!" cried Goldman, throwing his rolled up tie at the cat. Bacon sprang down and as he did so, Hymie caught sight of a large white envelope with his name embossed on it in gold letters, sitting on the top of his desk.

Inside was an invitation card which read:

'You are cordially invited to an extraordinary meeting of the Magic Triangle, tonight at midnight. Failure to attend may result in death.'

"Bloody magicians!" cried Hymie. This time he'd show them

where they could stick their dirty tricks. He opened his desk drawer and retrieved a pair of heavy brass knuckle dusters that Mike had given him for Christmas. He wasn't much cop at fighting, but sometimes there wasn't any choice.

Part Eleven

Like Lazarus

Mike awoke, tied to a wooden chair with electrical cable, in a dark dank basement, poorly lit by a single low wattage light-bulb hanging from the ceiling above his head. He could smell the river and assumed he was in a tunnel somewhere in London. His head felt groggy and his nose and shirt seemed to have dried blood on them, although for once he couldn't remember being in a fight. He flexed his giant shoulders but the chair only creaked while the cable threatened to cut off the blood supply to his triceps.

"Hello! Hello!" he shouted. "Where the hell am I?" His words reverberated around the walls. "It's not that new West End club they're all talking about is it? *The Sewer*? Well, the service is bloody awful!" he cried, more to cheer himself up than anything.

There was a muttering in the darkness and a shuffling of feet. Suddenly, a dwarf appeared dressed for a circus performance.

"Welcome to the Carnival of Fools, Mr Murphy, my name's Rimbono. Sorry about the blood on your shirt by the way, you were heavier than expected, I believe they dropped you."

"Don't mention it, Shorty. It looks like I'm the only one here; does that make me King of the Fools? That figures. I see you didn't invite my business partner, Hymie Goldman along. Now *he* knows a thing or two about fools."

Again, there was muttering in the darkness, followed by the shuffle of feet.

"He wasn't there when we collected you. At least, no one answering his description; just a client I suppose, a clean-shaven man wearing a tie."

Mike smiled. "Like you say, it couldn't have been Goldman. A right scruffy git he is."

"But, never fear, we left him an invitation to join us. After all, we didn't want the great Hymie Goldman to feel left out," added Rimbono.

"He's used to it," said Mike. He couldn't quite believe anyone would refer to Goldman as great, even for a laugh. "He won't come, you know; he hates parties."

"Oh, he'll come to this one," said the dwarf.

"So, if this is a party, where are the drinks and the cheesy nibbles?" asked Mike.

"All in good time," said the dwarf, removing five hand-grenades from the lining of his jacket and starting to juggle with them.

"I don't suppose you've heard of the *Carnival of Fools* before, have you?" continued the dwarf.

"No, it's not big in Finchley," said Mike.

"Hardly surprising, given that no one ever leaves it alive," said Rimbono for effect.

Suddenly another dwarf appeared from the shadows. He was identical to Rimbono and must have been his twin brother.

"We were going to call it the *Carnival of Death*, but thought it sounded a bit naff, weren't we dearie?" said the newcomer, in an effeminate, high pitched whine.

Rimbono glared at his brother. "You always have to butt in at the wrong time, don't you, Malvolio; like the ham actor you are!"

"Ooh, get her!" snapped Malvolio.

"Ladies, ladies, please," said Mike. "Not in front of strangers surely."

"Temper, temper, ducky. Still, they don't come much stranger than you, eh?" said Malvolio, giving their prisoner a cursory glance. "The name's Malvolio, matey, I'm famous. I've toured the world with all the *best* circuses as a juggler and acrobat; Malvolio the Magnificent they call me or Mal the Mag for short. He thinks he can juggle," he said, nodding at his brother, "but he can't!"

Mike looked blankly from one to the other.

"You *must* have heard of me," pleaded Malvolio.

Rimbono smirked.

"Nope…no, wait, yes, I *have,*" said Mike. "I read about you some place. That was it, I read about you in *Juggling Balls Monthly* – Val the Fag they called you. They said your act was shit!" he added.

Malvolio removed a flick-knife from his jacket pocket and extended the blade.

"I don't think I like you any more, sunshine," he said.

Rimbono was laughing quietly to himself now. "Wait, brother, we haven't asked him any questions yet," he said.

Malvolio glowered venomously at Mike and with an effort of will put away the knife. "Your witness, Bono," he said curtly.

Mike was still trying to work out what he was doing there. Okay, so he'd been drugged or hypnotised or something and they'd brought him to this dump, but why? What did they think he knew? And who were they anyway?

Rimbono began juggling his hand-grenades again. It clearly helped him to relax. Mike considered asking him if they were live or not but thought better of it.

The dwarf looked irritably at his brother again then turned to face Murphy, still writhing in his chair.

"Where's Harvey?" he asked.

The question seemed to take Mike by surprise. "Harvey who?" he queried instinctively.

"Don't play games with me, Murphy; *The Amazing Harvey*. He calls himself a magician, but he's really a spy," said Rimbono.

"A spy?" said Mike. "Are you sure?"

"Look, who's asking the questions here, dummy? Either you're trying to hold out on us or you really are as stupid as you seem. Neither makes much sense. You see, I only have to pull the pin on one of these babies and walk out of the room for a moment and you'll be plastered all over the walls, see?" said Rimbono.

Mike stared from one brother to the other, searching in vain for some trace of humanity. They looked like a couple of refugees from hell and he knew that if he didn't get out of there soon they would finish him for sure.

"Who are you working for, Murphy?" asked a voice from the darkness.

There was an intense pain behind Mike's eyes and he felt an overwhelming desire to answer any question they asked him. It was as though he were a tiny insect caught up in a maelstrom, powerless to resist the ebb and flow of life itself.

"Who's asking?" asked Mike.

"Watch the grenades, Murphy. Watch them as they spin round and round. Watch them as they suck your mind into the vortex." Rimbono smiled a sardonic grin at him in the ghastly half light as the projectiles blurred into an arc of destruction.

"The pain!" cried Murphy. "For God's sake stop it!"

"It will end as soon as you tell us what we want to know," said the voice in the darkness.

"Okay, okay. I'll tell you anything!" shouted Murphy.

"Who are you working for?"

"Redrum," said Mike.

"What's he look like?" asked his interrogator.

"I dunno, I've never met him," said Mike, "ask Hymie, he's met him. He could be anyone for all I know. He could even be you."

The third man appeared from the shadows, an ominous presence of a man concealed behind a black cape.

"He could indeed, as you say, be me," said the man in a strange Eurasian accent. "But, of course, he isn't. Now, tell me about *The Amazing Harvey*; where does he live? Where does he hang out? Who are his known associates?"

"I've told you, I don't know!" cried Mike.

He slumped forward in his chair and tried again to loosen the cable binding him to the chair. The pain in his head was excruciating. He bit down hard on his lower lip until he drew blood. The sudden burst of pain in his mouth inexplicably helped clear the fog in his brain.

Any normal man waking from a nightmare, who found himself strapped to a chair and being interrogated by shadows and dwarves might despair, might give in to the encroaching madness and lose the will to live. Alone and in the dark, Michael Aloysius Murphy was different to others; no better no worse, just less inclined to quit and more inclined to fight.

"Look, I've had enough of this. I don't know who you think you are but there are laws against kidnapping and torture in this country, mush, and when I get out of here I'm gonna push your face so far down your neck you'll be eating out of your backside!" cried Murphy.

Mike's giant frame twisted and contorted like a huge serpent caught in the jaws of an enormous crocodile.

Snap! Crackle! Crunch!

The wooden chair disintegrated into splintered fragments beneath him as Mike stood up, several pieces of broken chair still hanging from his nether regions.

"Oh shit!" exclaimed Rimbono, who froze mid-juggle and watched in horror as the grenades landed one after the other with a metallic clang on the basement floor. All but the last, which fell into Mike's outstretched palm. He pulled the pin and held on tightly to the release clip with his strong, thick fingers.

The dwarves had already started running for the exit.

"Thanks, morons, I was trying to find out how to get out of here!" cried Mike.

He turned around to look at his arch-inquisitor, the man in the shadows, but there was no one there.

"Oh well, waste not want not," said Mike, throwing the grenade into the darkness at the far end of the room before running as fast as he could in the opposite direction.

Part Twelve

Too young to live, too old to die

At ten minutes to midnight, Hymie Goldman sat ashen faced on the bus to Euston station. He'd never make it, they hadn't given him enough time, but if anything happened to Mike, he'd never live with himself. Who else would do all the dangerous, boring jobs? You just couldn't find people willing to take them on. Mike was irreplaceable.

Outside the bus, neon-flecked tourists and drunken revellers jostled with late night commuters on their way to the late night kebab shop. London was no place for the old, the slow, the weak or the poor, and though Goldman permed three from four he had a steely, purposeful look in his eye for once. Damn it, the big guy needed him and how often did that happen?

"Eh, mate, got 50p for the bus?" asked the bearded semi-vagrant in the seat behind him.

"You're already on the bus, you scrounging git! What are you trying to do, save up and buy one?!" snapped Hymie.

A two-tone paper flyer, lying discarded on the floor at his feet, caught his attention. He picked it up and straightened out the creases.

'Marvo the Magnificent performs his death defying bullet catching feat for one night only. Thursday 7th at the Jack Raddish Memorial theatre in the Novotel, Hammersmith. Be there. Be amazed. Tickets £10 from all good agencies.'

Maybe he'd know Harvey? It was worth a try.

Several minutes later the bus ground to a halt at Euston and

Hymie hopped off before the other passengers could alight. As he headed along the pavement towards Stephenson Way, he suddenly noticed a glow in the sky and a cloud of black smoke rising in a column above the street he was heading for. He started to run. Within a few yards he developed a stitch in his side but he continued running through the pain. Mike would do no less for him and he could be in that building.

A fire engine rushed past, its siren blaring in the calm night air.

Hymie followed it at a distance as it turned into Stephenson Way. When he got close enough to see for himself, he was struck dumb at the appalling sight before him. The Magic Triangle building had been reduced to a pile of steaming rubble. He ran across the road to the cordon barriers. Flames flickered amidst the ruins. Charred timbers, posters and leather bound books smouldered on all sides and the battered entrance sign emblazoned with the Triangle's motto, *Age tuum negotium,* lay disregarded in the wreckage.

"Mike! Mike!! Where the hell are you?"

Goldman covered his mouth with a tatty handkerchief and closed his eyes to keep out the smoke fumes, but also to blot out the thought that no one inside the building could have survived that explosion.

"Dear God, bring him back! Don't let the great lummox die. I swear on my mother's life I'll never expect him to do all the crappy jobs again!" cried Goldman morosely into the cacophony of wailing sirens.

He couldn't get close enough to the building's main entrance to see anything so he skirted around the block to the rear entrance, which hadn't been quite so utterly destroyed.

He was about to leave in the vague hope that Mike had been down the pub or out on the town with that Greek bird, Bazookas, when Hymie noticed a rather tatty boot sticking out of a pile of rubble, and thought he'd better investigate.

He dug around the boot until a large hairy leg emerged, then clawed and scrabbled at the earth and shattered timbers with mounting excitement and fear. Could this person still be alive? Would they know what had happened to Mike or why the building had been so totally devastated? He continued to dig.

As he continued to dig, Hymie came across a large piece of door pressing down across the top half of the poor devil. He lifted it with great difficulty before realising that there was a concealed air pocket beneath it and that it had probably saved this guy's life.

The man was filthy and covered in ash but as the door came off his face he suddenly coughed and spluttered into life.

"Huuuuurrrgh!"

"You've had a lucky escape, mate," said Hymie.

"You could have fooled me! Where the hell have you been, Goldman?"

"Mike?"

"Well, who were you expecting? The Amazing Bloody Harvey?"

"It's great to see you… I thought you were dead," said Hymie.

"What? And let you get my share of the dosh!" quipped Mike.

"Same old Mike. I'll get us a cab back to the office and you can tell me all about it before you pass out."

Part Thirteen

Clouds over Hammersmith

After a week of incoherent babbling about dwarves and men with no face, Mike was ready for a big night out and Hymie needed a change of scene, so they headed for the Novotel, Hammersmith with something verging on enthusiasm.

Outside, the letter 'v' in the green neon lit sign appeared to have fused, leaving Hammersmith's only 'No.otel' looking somewhat sorry for itself.

The detective duo pushed past the revolving door and headed for the concierge's desk, where a bored looking twenty-something was yawning and reading the local paper.

"Can I help you?" he asked.

"We've come for the big show," said Hymie.

"Right...er, would that be the International Parrot Fancier's Convention or the Magician?"

Mike looked bewildered at the reply. His life was getting stranger by the day and the last thing he needed was a run in with a bunch of exotic birds.

"The Magician, of course," said Hymie. "I saw a flyer for it; Marvo the Magnificent and his amazing bullet catching act."

"Oh, you want the Jack Raddish," said the concierge.

"I beg your pardon, sunshine," said Mike. "We came here to see a magician, not some prawn named after a salad."

"It's the name of the theatre," hissed Hymie, out of the corner of his mouth.

"Yes, up two flights of stairs and along to the West Wing," said the concierge, picking up his paper again.

They headed into the voluminous interior of the building in search of the Jack Raddish Memorial Theatre, and hoped it had a bar.

"They're big on overblown stage names aren't they," said Mike.

"Magicians?" confirmed Hymie.

"Yeah, who else, you nurk; *The Amazing Harvey, Marvo the Magnificent*…you never come across one called average Sid or plain Bob, do you?"

Hymie just smiled. When Mike was in his pseudo philosophic mood, you just had to let him talk it off.

"I suppose it's the posters…" continued Mike.

"Eh?" said Hymie, trying in vain to maintain the intellectual level of the conversation.

"Well, who's gonna go to see some bloke called Bob doing magic tricks? You just wouldn't bother would you? On the other hand, there's that guy…what's he called? Dave? No, Darren…that's it, Darren Brown. He's a big name these days even though he sounds like someone from down the pub."

"Actually, it's Derren," said Hymie.

"What, Darren Derren? Shows all you know, Goldman; sounds more like the Pink Panther theme tune."

"Have it your way, mate," said Hymie, handing the tickets he'd bought the previous afternoon to the usherette.

She smiled hesitantly at him. "I've been asked to let all patrons know that there's an escaped African Grey in the auditorium," she said.

"African Grey what?" asked Mike, with visions of elephants, rhinoceri and herds of wildebeest stampeding through the front stalls.

"Parrot," said the girl. "He's escaped from the International Parrot Fanciers Doodah," she added, by way of explanation, "but he's not dangerous."

"Not as dangerous as the fanciers anyway," quipped Hymie.

"They should have caught him before curtain up," said the girl.

"The fanciers should have been locked up years ago," added Hymie.

They walked down the aisle and took their seats, shuffling along row G past an irascible woman in a turquoise hat and a fat man with gravy spots down his tie. A recorded drum roll crackled over the PA system and the purple satin curtains parted to reveal a short, smartly dressed man with thinning hair and his tall, statuesque assistant, a blonde girl in her thirties who looked stunning in her gold lamé dress and fishnet stockings.

"Ladies and Gentlemen," continued the voice on the tannoy. "For one night only as part of his world tour, please give a big Jack Raddish welcome to the one, the only, the legendary…Marvo the Magnificent."

Three people clapped.

Marvo the Magnificent, or Bob Evans as he was known down *The Goat and Compasses*, looked a little under-whelmed. Nevertheless, he strode manfully to the front of the stage to address his audience.

"Ladies, Gents, Children, it's a great pleasure to be here performing for you tonight en route to the Hippodrome, Bradford. In a moment, I will perform the feat known to audiences around the world as the bullet catching trick; a trick which is as difficult and as dangerous to perform as any before seen on the magic circuit. But first, please put your hands together for my assistants this evening, the lovely Lavinia…"

The girl in the golden getup took an elegant bow, displaying her magnificent cleavage to the men in the plastic macs in the front row and generating an enthusiastic applause.

Up in the fly loft there was an audible squawking sound and a few grey feathers fluttered down onto the stage.

"…and ace marksman, Hugo Herschel," concluded Marvo.

A dapper man in a hunting jacket with a handlebar moustache appeared from the wings and took a bow. The applause continued in a lower key.

The noise seemed to disturb Einstein, the African Grey parrot, who had been resting above the stage and he flew out towards the back of the auditorium showering the audience below with bird droppings.

The lady with the turquoise hat took a direct hit and Mike was spattered with white splashes of bird muck across the shoulders of his jacket.

The woman stood up in disgust. "Someone call for the manager, this is an absolute disgrace!" she cried.

"Perhaps Hugo can shoot that bloody bird!" shouted a heckler from the back.

Marvo beamed and directed his gaze at the lady with the ruined hat.

"I'm afraid Hugo would get into serious trouble if he started taking pot shots at poor defenceless birds. Never mind, dear lady, I'm sure the manager will recompense you for the damage. As for me, I can only sympathise," he said, pulling a bouquet of flowers from his jacket sleeve and passing them across the orchestra pit to her. He gestured to an attendant at the back of the auditorium for someone to capture the parrot.

"And now, ladies and gentlemen," continued Marvo. "Moving on to an illusion many have attempted but few survived, please be silent while I perform my world famous bullet catching act." He nodded to Lavinia, then walked to the centre of the stage and sat down on a specially prepared bar stool. Lavinia shimmied across the stage after him and then tied a specially prepared blindfold over his eyes.

"You will see, ladies and gentlemen, that I can see nothing of what may be about to happen," said Marvo.

The audience sat in hushed silence as ace marksman Hugo walked to a specially prepared spot on the stage and, removing a Smith and Wesson revolver from its case, carefully checked that it was loaded.

It was so quiet you could have heard a pin drop.

"Uh oh," said Einstein the parrot, from somewhere over the audience's heads, as two men in white coats approached him with a net.

A few members of the audience laughed nervously.

"Lavinia, if you please," said Marvo the Magnificent.

She pulled the cord on a small curtain which fell open to reveal a large stopwatch, mounted on a wooden board.

"When the countdown commences, I will have precisely sixty seconds of life left before Hugo pulls the trigger on that gun and we shall see, once and for all, if I really *can* catch a bullet in my teeth," said Marvo.

Lavinia pressed the release button on the clock and it began its countdown, every second audibly ticking away.

Marvo ran his tongue over the edge of the spent bullet inside his mouth and counted down the seconds, as he had done so many times before in rehearsal. To make his death appear authentic he had to take the dive at exactly the moment Hugo fired the blank round at him.

The seconds sounded out in Marvo's head as the time ebbed away on the clock. Thirty seconds, twenty, ten. His leg muscles braced themselves to flick the stool forwards as he prepared to fling himself backwards across the stage. Five seconds, four, three, two, one.

BANG!!

The audience collectively seemed to stop breathing as they focused on the motionless figure stretched out before them on the stage. Marvo's arm twitched and the audience erupted through sheer relief into a thunderous applause.

Lavinia walked across the stage to the prostrate figure of Marvo to help him to his feet for his curtain call, but then stopped suddenly, her face etched with shock and dread. She signalled to the stagehand to lower the curtain and fell to her knees at Marvo's feet. He was bleeding badly and incoherent with shock.

"Bob, Bob! Can you hear me? What happened?" she implored him, leaning across his blood-soaked jacket to hear whatever he had to say.

He opened his mouth to speak but only managed to utter a couple of words before sinking back to the ground with dull and lifeless eyes.

Lavinia ran backstage, tears streaming down her face.

"Call the manager, he's dead! Marvo's dead," she cried.

Even on the other side of the curtain it was increasingly obvious to the audience that something was wrong. No one performed a magic act like that without taking a large number of elaborate bows. Was Marvo injured? Was he *dead*? Surely they had all seen him move, surely he had to be alive, but if so, where was he?

By the time the news broke, the audience were queuing to get out.

Goldman, having been in more scrapes than most, had the presence of mind to get to the front of the queue.

"They're gonna lock us in and call the police, Mike. They're gonna need witness statements and that's the last place we need to be," he said, running for the exit before the manager could lock the doors. He oh so nearly made it.

"Hold on a minute, mate, where do you think you're going?" It was the assistant deputy relief bar manager, Dave Parsons.

Hymie drew himself up to his full five feet six inches and let him have it with both barrels.

"Ah, Mr…Parsnips," he said, giving the manager's badge a cursory glance, "I'm Arnold Stockhausen and this is my colleague, Kevin Fishbone," he added, pointing to a large man covered in bird shit who was rapidly approaching up the staircase. "We're from the Institute of Applied Parrot Studies. I was about to contact the RSPCB, the Freedom for Parrots League and the Health and Safety Executive about the worst case of parrot mishandling I've ever seen," added Hymie, "but if you let us out of the back door I may just be able to content myself with a strongly worded letter to the Parrot Breeders Gazette."

Dave Parsons' face fell. As aghast as he was at this tirade of verbal diarrhoea, he couldn't for the life of him think of anything appropriate to say and it was while his face was working overtime that Mike seized his chance and knocked him out of the way with a smart left hook.

Parsons fell to the ground like a sack of spuds and Goldman and Murphy hastily retreated from 'Novohell' the way they had come. Strolling along Hammersmith Broadway a few moments later, they happened upon two familiar faces hurrying along in the direction they had just come.

"Good God! It's Hymie Goldman," cried Inspector Decca.

"And Mike Birdshit," added Sergeant Terse sarcastically.

Mike glowered at him, but had learnt when to hold his tongue.

"Well, they always did have trouble with the birds," said Decca, laughing.

"Evening, Inspector," said Hymie. "Going somewhere nice are we?"

"Now that would be telling, Goldman," said Decca. "I only hope you're not mixed up in it though."

"What? Us, Inspector?" said Mike.

"We keep a very low profile these days," concurred Hymie, as the two detectives made a beeline for the nearest cab rank out of there.

★

After a couple of hours of taking witness statements at the Novotel, Hammersmith, Decca and Terse managed to find some other mugs to finish the job while they returned to the police station for a supposed meeting with the Chief.

As they entered Decca's new office on the second floor of Metropolitan House, the phone started ringing.

"Get that would you Terse, I can't face any more pointless conversations this evening."

Terse nodded and lifted the receiver. "Inpector Decca's office; Sergeant Terse speaking."

"Can I speak to Ray Decca please, it's urgent."

Terse handed over the receiver. "It's urgent" he whispered.

"Hello, Decca here, who's speaking please?"

"About bloomin' time mate, I've been calling you for hours. It's Terry Longbottom, your ex-wife's new partner. Your central heating boiler has just packed up and I wanted to know who to call to get it repaired. I presume you have a comprehensive service agreement?"

"I see," said Decca, retaining his composure with some difficulty. "Well, Mr Large Bottom, I should call the Samaritans if I were you, because if you call me at work again I will personally see to it that the boiler's pipework is inserted so far up your arse that you have steam coming out of your ears permanently. Go boil your head!" snapped Decca, almost smashing the receiver as he laid it to rest on his desk.

"Trouble at home, guv?" asked the sergeant.

"Nothing I can't handle, Terse. They must think I'm soft in the head," said Decca.

"Who, sir? The Gas Board?"

Ray Decca smiled sadly and sat down behind his desk.

"So, Terse, what did you make of this evening's events?"

The sergeant scratched his head briefly then sat down in the visitor's chair facing his boss.

"Well, sir, it's a funny business really. I've investigated plenty of homicides, but not where the victim was shot on stage in front of three hundred witnesses. At least it looks like an open and shut case; Marvo's assistant, Hugo Herschel was seen by the entire audience shooting him at point blank range. Everyone assumed the bullet he fired was a blank but it obviously wasn't. Why he did it we don't know, but perhaps he'll come clean when he thinks it over. Perhaps he'll plead guilty to manslaughter. Maybe it was just some terrible accident," said Sergeant Terse.

"Or maybe Herschel was just the patsy," said Decca. "Maybe when we look into it further the other assistant, Lavinia, stood to gain financially from Marvo's death."

"Yeah, maybe it was an insurance scam," added Terse. He stared momentarily into space before continuing. "But what I don't get were his last words."

"His last words?" queried Decca.

"Not Bolton."

"Are you serious, Sergeant? Marvo's last words were *not Bolton*?" asked Decca, perplexed.

"Straight up, guv. That's what that Lavinia bird said," added Terse.

"So, were they due to perform in Bolton? Was there someone there with a grudge against him?" asked Decca, intrigued.

"That's the funny thing, guv, she definitely said that they weren't appearing in Bolton."

"Well, he won't be now, that's for sure," added Decca.

"The other thing that got me thinking, sir, was that it was way too much of a coincidence to run into Goldman and Murphy coming away from the crime scene when we arrived."

"You know, Terse, I think we'll make a detective of you yet," said Inspector Decca. "Come on, Barry, let's pay them a little social visit on the way to the curry house."

Part Fourteen

Puzzled of Finchley

It was late when Hymie and Mike got back to 792A Finchley Road after the concert. The lengthening shadows of dusk had departed, to be replaced by dark streets sporadically lit by the neon glow of the all-night mini-mart and the Taj Mahal curry house, successor to Benny Baker's celebrated Pizzeria.

Hymie tore off a calling card which had been attached to the weather-beaten woodwork of their front door with a nail-gun and squinted at it.

"Madame Za Za. Whether you're a giant or a dwarf, I'm the medium for you," he read aloud.

Mike chuckled. "A charlatan with a sense of humour," he said.

"Don't knock what you don't understand, Mike. I've been thinking we should contact a spirit medium for a while now," said Hymie.

"Well, I suppose they can't be any worse than your usual method; sticking the names of all the suspects on a dartboard and throwing darts at it until you hit one."

Hymie scowled. "You're only jealous. At least I *have* a method," he said.

Once inside their squalid office, North London's second worst detectives broke open a bottle of Tizer and stretched out in their decrepit armchairs to piece together another seemingly insoluble puzzle.

Bacon the cat strolled casually across the room as though he owned the place and curled up on the moth-eaten settee, where he proceeded to lick his balls meticulously.

Hymie looked on in mute fascination.

"Okay, Mike, what do *you* make of this case?" he asked.

"I dunno, it's the strangest case I've ever seen and I've only ever worked with you, so strange is normal," said Mike. "You've got more chance of filling out your tax return correctly than cracking this one, Goldman."

"Tax returns? Hah, I don't have time to waste on that mindless bureaucracy. It's just gibberish submitted by the gullible to the unemployable who don't understand what they're looking at when they get it. Besides, we have accountants for all that crap."

"We have *accountants*?" asked Mike, impressed. "Who the heck are they?" he asked as an afterthought.

Hymie's brain started racing while he cast a furtive glance around the room for inspiration.

"Oh, Furball and Mildew," he replied as his eyes alighted on the cat and the shambolic decor.

"That figures," said Mike. "I bet we've got Mildew."

"Speak for yourself," said Hymie. "Oh, they may not be the biggest or the best firm around these parts," he continued, "but at least they show that we're legit. We're respectable businessmen not penny ante sharks like some of the cowboys around here."

"Leaving aside how, or whether, we pay Bodgett and Scarper for their creative accounting, how *are* we going to solve this case, Goldman?"

"Mike, Mike, you worry too much. I've been thinking it over. Nothing could be simpler, we'll just tell Redrum that *The Amazing Harvey* has emigrated..."

"Yeah, to Russia," said Mike. "It might work."

"Russia? Niet, who's gonna believe that? I was thinking of France," said Hymie.

"Why? Do they like rotten magic acts over there? Pick a card, any card, monsieur, it doesn't matter which one 'cause they're all the Jacque of 'earts!"

"Listen, Mush," said Hymie. "It just needs to be somewhere Redrum might *believe* Harvey might actually want to go. If he did his magic show in Moscow he'd either freeze his balls off or actually perform the flamin' act somewhere and wind up with a concrete overcoat at the bottom of the river Volga."

"It's not gonna cut it, is it, Hymie? Redrum's not your normal client you can blag with stories about how you *nearly* found the missing magician but he got away. He's gonna be after us with a semi automatic and no one even knows what he looks like or where he lives. Even I'm a bit nervous about the guy and I don't scare easy," said Mike.

"Okay, I get it," said Hymie, "but that's not the only option on the table is it?"

"Glad to hear it," said Mike.

Hymie scratched his head. He needed more time, more money, a new life.

"Let's just re-cap on the facts so far," he said, dispiritedly.

"If you think it will help," said Mike.

"From the top," said Hymie. "We were hired by some guy calling himself Redrum, who's publicity shy to say the least. In fact we've never seen his face."

"Perhaps he's a she, maybe he's a woman," said Mike.

"Yeah, it's the way he walks," said Hymie, sarcastically. "Or maybe he has some instantly recognisable feature like a birthmark or a scar or a tattoo which he needs to keep hidden," he added, bulldozing Mike's theory out of the way. "So, what have we got, Mike? A rubbish magician," said Hymie, writing 'Harvey' in red marker pen on the wall. "What else?"

"The Magic Triangle?" queried Mike, dubiously.

"OK," said Hymie, writing 'Triangle' on the wall beneath the first clue.

"Anything else?" asked Hymie.

"What about that ruddy parrot," said Mike. "I've never seen so much bird shit in one place in all my life as down my jacket after that show."

Hymie stared distractedly into space for a moment before writing 'full of shit' at the bottom of the wall.

"OK, Goldman, what does it all add up to?"

Hymie cleared his throat and read the list of clues from the top, "Harvey Triangle full of shit." He looked mildly disappointed as though he'd half expected it to make sense. "What do you make of it, Mike?"

"I dunno, but while we're sitting around playing silly buggers, half the Magic Triangle are being snuffed out by a bunch of homicidal maniacs," said Mike. "It's no wonder we can't find this Harvey geezer; if he's got any sense he's probably keeping his head down to stay alive. We should just give Redrum his money back and lie low for a while."

"I can't see him letting us go now," said Hymie. "Even if we had the money left to pay him back," he sighed.

"Are there any more vital statistics we've missed, Einstein?" asked Mike.

"Ruby," said Hymie, with a wistful glint in his eye. "It stands to reason she's mixed up in this somewhere. No one quits a job after one day of making tea."

"You did. Remember when you were an electrician?"

"Thank you very much, Michael. You had to bring that up, didn't you? Well, all that was a very long time ago. Still, there's no such thing as coincidence. If a bloke breaks wind in Kuala Lumpur you can be sure there'll be a typhoon in Tahiti before long."

"So who's been guffing in here then?" asked Mike.

Hymie took a swig from his glass with a pained expression on his face. "Probably that bloody cat," he added.

"So what do we do now?" asked Mike.

Hymie reflected. Why on earth would Ruby be involved? She was no criminal, just a normal girl looking for a normal job. She'd just taken a long hard look at him and their crummy offices and decided to take a better offer. Any offer, probably.

"I dunno," said Hymie quietly. "I wish she'd come back with those cakes, though," he added. "I could just murder one now."

Mike nodded in agreement.

"OK, Mike, let's go over it all again. What have we got? A guy who hates magicians? He certainly hates Harvey. What if he also bumped off that magician in Wood Green?"

"Marvin?" suggested Mike.

"Yeah, and Marvo the Magnificent," continued Hymie.

"But why?" asked Mike. "I can't stand that crappy talent contest show on the telly but I don't go around popping off the contestants and panellists do I?"

"No, but you're not a homicidal maniac," said Hymie.

"True, true," said Mike. "So we're looking for a homicidal maniac with a grudge against magicians."

"Very possibly," said Hymie, wondering if that was such a good idea.

"But how the hell are we ever going to find him?" asked Mike, returning to the nub of the matter like an overgrown terrier.

"Maybe it's time to involve the police," said Hymie. "We could use some protection."

"What from Decca and Terse?" queried Mike. "They'd probably just stand by laughing while we got wasted."

Hymie picked up the calling card he'd discarded on the table by the door. "Then we'd better speak to Madame Za Za. I'll call her, there's no time to lose."

"You're nuts, Goldman, completely bonkers, mate! Why don't you just read your freakin' tea-leaves or something?"

"Everyone needs an edge in this game, Murphy and you'd be surprised how many great detectives work with psychics."

"Yeah, just before they get carted off to the nuthouse, mate. We could always go undercover again," said Mike, trying to avoid the inevitable. "Set ourselves up as a magic act and see if we can draw Redrum's fire," he added.

"Count me out, Murphy. It's not that I'm chicken or anything," said Hymie, unconvincingly. "It's just that I don't look good in fishnet tights and you'd make an even worse-looking assistant than me. Besides, how on earth would we get any bookings?"

The phone on Hymie's desk started ringing.

"Look's like they've heard about our magic act already," said Hymie, lifting the receiver.

"Goldman and Murphy, Magicians," he said.

"Good grief! Is that you, Mr Goldman?" It was a woman's voice; the voice of a woman used to getting her own way.

"Sod it, it's that Flanagan woman again," hissed Hymie, away from the phone. He lifted the receiver again.

"Solly, Chinese Laundree shut!" he cried, in his best Widow Twankey voice, before slamming down the handset.

Mike had wandered across to the window and was peering through the yellowed blinds.

"Unless you wanna spend the rest of the night down at Fuzz Central explaining to Decca and Terse what we were doing at the Hammersmith Novotel while a murder was being committed, I suggest we get outta here fast," said Mike.

The phone started ringing again.

"Quick, to the fire escape!" cried Hymie.

"I didn't know there was one," said Mike.

"Well, not as such, but the builders never took that bit of old scaffolding down when they repaired next door's roof last month and beggars can't be choosers," said Hymie, beating a hasty retreat out of the rear window.

Part Fifteen

Fuzzy Night

They came from far and wide, from the four corners of the metropolis; the greatest assemblage of senior police officers ever collected in one place, not for some must-see event, rather on pain of demotion and exclusion from the Met's inner circle.

Noone could remember the last time there had been a triple red alert, so they were all a bit sketchy about the protocol, but they all knew without any shadow of a doubt that they had to attend, come what may. Deep in the bowels of New Scotland Yard, in the lead-lined room with the biological warfare sign on the door, the Deputy Chief Constable, Jack Robinson, MBE, GCSE, NURK, stood at the lectern at the end of the gallery and tapped his baton for silence. A panel of the great and the good sat alongside him, screwing up their eyes to make out the faces of the assembled masses under the low wattage emergency lighting.

"Gentlemen, lady," began the Chief. "We are facing a major threat which I need your full support and cooperation to deal with. As you will know from recent incident reports and in the media, there have been a spate of attacks on members of the Magic Triangle. Only last week their headquarters in Euston were blown up and several of their members have been murdered. I need hardly say that this is no coincidence and we believe the Triangle's old adversary, the Red Square is resurgent."

"What evidence is there?" asked a senior officer from the back of the room.

"The statistics are revealing in themselves," continued DCC Robinson. "Of the 365 registered members of the Triangle, fifteen have died in suspicious circumstances in the last six months and many of the others have disappeared without a trace. The Grand Wizard himself, J R Bowling, called me up a few days ago from his bunker in the Edinburgh suburbs to warn me that the Triangle could face extinction before the all important Police Ball season."

"Balls!"

"Who said that?" snapped DCI Donkin, a dinosaur of urban policing who'd survived numerous allegations of police brutality, as he struck the desk in front of him repeatedly with a six inch length of lead pipe he just happened to have about him.

"It was DI Cavanagh, sir, he's got Tourette's," explained an officer seated in the front row. "It's the new legislation, we're not allowed to ask about health issues at interview any longer and the interview panel just thought he was refreshingly forthright."

The Chief rolled his eyes to where heaven should have been then turned back reluctantly to face the desk wrecker.

"That'll do, Donkin. That desk is coming out of your budget by the way," added DCC Robinson.

"Hah!" replied Donkin, hitting the desk once more for luck from force of habit.

"No, what I meant was; how do we know it was the Red Triangle?" asked the officer at the back of the room.

"Who the blazes are they anyway?" asked Donkin. "Red Triangle my arse, they sound like a right bunch of plonkers!"

"Gentlemen, DCI Perkins," resumed the Chief, smiling apologetically at the only female officer in the room, "this is intolerable. There are magicians out there being systematically wiped off the face of the map and all we can do is sit around scratching our…"

"Balls!" cried Cavanagh.

"Heads," concluded the Chief.

"Are we sure we're not dealing with a serial killer?" continued the officer at the back.

"Who said that?" asked DCC Robinson. "I can't see you very well from here."

"DI O'Connor, sir," replied the faceless one.

"No relation to Lord O'Connor I suppose?"

"He's my father," replied the officer.

"A *very* good question, O'Connor," said DCC Robinson. "But I think we can rule out a serial killer for three good reasons. Would anyone like to name them?"

"Bloody Cornflakes!" snapped Cavanagh.

Robinson turned briefly to Donkin. "Get him out of here," he hissed before continuing with the briefing. Donkin headed off with a purposeful glint in his bloodshot eyes.

"Firstly, fifteen homicides in six months seems too high for one killer. It's not like some madman has gone on the rampage in a shopping centre, these murders were all carefully planned and executed. Secondly, if it *were* one perpetrator then we believe it's more likely we'd have some corroborating evidence from the various crime scenes; the same gun or modus operandi. As it is, we have practically nothing to go on; no credible suspects, no witnesses, nothing."

"And thirdly, sir?" asked O'Connor.

"Third? Did I say *three* reasons? Ah…yes…well."

There was a distant thudding of boots down the corridor outside, then the door flew open and Inspector Ray Decca appeared before the assembled masses, panting for breath and with a battered videotape in his hand.

"I was asked to give you this, Chief," he said to DCC Robinson.

An officer in the front row took the tape from him and, flicking a couple of red switches on the communications console in the central isle, inserted the tape into it.

The tape began to roll. A grainy image of two dishevelled characters flickered across the screen above their heads. They appeared to be making a hasty getaway from a burning building.

"This film was taken by CCTV on the night the Magic Triangle's headquarters were blown up," said Decca.

"Does anyone recognise those two men?" asked DCC Robinson.

There was a non-committal mumbling across the room.

"I do, sir," said Decca. "I'd recognise them anywhere. I know them like the back of my hand. The large gorilla in the smouldering donkey jacket is a former bouncer called Mike Murphy and the short scruffy one is his partner in crime, Hymie Goldman."

"Good work, Decca. Bring them in for questioning," said the Chief.

Decca smiled. "Leave it to me, sir" he said. He headed back towards the entrance in a daze. He was back from the brink and this time he was back for good. You couldn't keep a good man down for long and they didn't come any better than Inspector Ray Decca.

Part Sixteen

AAAAA Cars for the discerning mug

On exiting Hendon tube station, if you hang a right then take a couple of lefts then perhaps another right and finally another left for luck, you could find yourself outside AAAAA Cars, just like Hymie did one cold and frosty morning. Having had enough of being treated like a sardine on public transport, of the timetables that made no sense and to which no self-respecting bus or train driver adhered anyway, Goldman had decided that enough was enough and he had to have his own wheels again. Yes, it was time to buy a car; a car that made a statement about him and who he was: that he was a class act, powerful, majestic and dignified; a tall order on £7,500.

Contrary to rumours, AAAAA Cars wasn't named after the punters who awoke screaming in the night once they realised what a heap of junk their cars were, but in the hope that they would appear first in any directory of car vendors daft enough to include them. Most people either called them 'Five–A' or tried not to mention them at all.

Five-A operated the kind of disorganised, sprawling forecourt that at first sight could have belonged to a scrap metal dealer. But the similarities didn't end there; if you couldn't see the vehicle of your dreams it was probably there somewhere, in bits, most likely, awaiting re-assembly to order. Hymie gave up looking after a perfunctory tour of the yard and headed into the low-rise 1950's pre-fab that passed as Five-A's office. Inside he was greeted, with complete indifference, by a man in his late twenties in a cheap suit and electric yellow tie. The office was old and tired looking with scruffy MDF furniture. Hymie felt right at home.

"Alright?" said the youth.

"Yes, I rang yesterday and spoke to a Mr Harris," said Hymie. "He said he could get me a collectable classic car at a price I could afford. The name's Goldman, Hymie Goldman."

"That's right, it was me," said Mr Harris, holding out his hand. "Paul Harris. How much *can* you afford?" he asked, hastily withdrawing his hand before Hymie had a chance to shake it.

"Well, er…" said Hymie, totting up an imaginary budget on his fingers. "Not a penny more than £7,500" he confided.

'That much!' thought Paul Harris, whistling discouragingly through his teeth. This Goldman character didn't exactly reek of money, but seven and a half grand wasn't to be sneezed at. "It won't be easy," he said, "but my word is my bond."

"Yes, Paul," began Hymie, "I see myself behind the wheel of a Bugatti, something in racing red with go faster stripes."

"With seven and a half grand I'm afraid you couldn't afford the steering wheel, let alone a whole car, but I may be able to get you a damaged hood ornament or a wing-mirror," said Harris, trying to inject a lethal dose of reality into Hymie's fantasy.

"Oh, right," said Goldman, "I didn't realise," he added. "So what do you have in my price range?"

"Well, Hymie, how about a classic American sedan?" asked the salesman, trying to remember where he'd left the old two-tone rust bucket. "You'd have the birds jumping all over you," he schmoozed. "They love those massive yet compact, stylish yet functional, comfortable yet sporty, models."

Hymie, who'd already begun to worry about the fuel consumption and how he was going to park something as vast as a classic American car, was immediately taken with the idea of being a hit with the ladies and raised the white flag.

"When can I see it?" he asked, eagerly.

"Well, it's not that simple, I'm afraid," said Paul Harris. "It's currently owned by a well known international rock star who I can't name for legal reasons. He's a household name though and has a genuine reason for selling. If you'd like to see a picture of the car, I can show it to you on my computer," he said, calling up a grainy image with a few quick key strokes.

Hymie squinted at the image then thought of the birds and the rock star life. "How many miles does it have on the clock?" he asked, for the sake of appearances.

Harris pressed another couple of buttons on his keypad. "237,000 genuine miles," he said.

"And how many non-genuine ones?" asked Hymie, suspiciously.

"Believe me, Hymie, that's nothing. This car's a 1969 Fleetwood with an 8.2 litre engine. It'll practically run forever. Ask Bon...oh, sorry, I shouldn't have said that," said Paul Harris; suggesting plenty without actually saying anything.

"How much is it?" asked Hymie, his resistance crumbling.

"Well, he wanted £10K for it but I haggled him down. It was hard work getting him to lower the price but I finally got him to agree to..."

"£7,500" said Hymie, holding out an envelope full of readies.

"Done," said Paul Harris, taking it from him. "Just pop your address down on this piece of paper and we'll get it delivered with the keys and log book in next to no time."

Part Seventeen

A kick in the crystal balls

The stars shone down reluctantly on the dark streets of North Finchley as Mike and Hymie embarked on their quest for enlightenment. Hymie remained convinced that a trip to Madame Za Za's would shed new light on the case, while Mike just couldn't think of a good enough reason to change Goldman's mind or to get out of going himself. Setting out on foot again with only the prospect of public transport for relief made Hymie wish all the more for the arrival of their new car, but as the delivery date was uncertain he didn't think Mike would appreciate the good news just yet. He would have to pick his moment to tell him.

Trouble lurked in the shadows around every nook and cranny for those foolhardy enough to seek it and as usual, the fool Goldman and the poor man's Oliver Hardy, Mike Murphy, fit the bill.

"Are you sure you want to do this, Goldman?" asked Mike, as though checking his colleague were sure he wanted a kick in the bollocks.

"I mean, most mediums are a bunch of con-artists who spin you a load of old tosh that on closer inspection could mean practically anything."

"Have faith, Mike. When have I ever let you down?" asked Hymie.

"How long have you got?" said Mike.

"Lately, I mean" added Hymie, to forestall yet another pointless bickering session.

"Besides, we don't have many other alleyways to explore at the moment."

As the words left Goldman's mouth, a tall shadowy figure in a cape emerged from a nearby side-street.

"I thought I'd find you here," said the stranger ominously.

"Ah, Mr Redrum," replied Hymie, nervously. "I was just about to call you."

"Call me what?" asked Redrum.

"Never mind," said Hymie.

"I thought I'd spare you the trouble, Goldman. Do you know the whereabouts of *The Amazing Harvey* or are you going to give me my money back?" he asked calmly.

Who do you think I am, Victor Kiam? thought Hymie "We're very close to finding him," he said hastily. "Another week, perhaps two…" He glanced at the expressionless mask of the stranger for some hint of a reaction. "Or perhaps just a few days …" he added. "We've looked under most of the usual stones but it's hard to tell. Still, we'll get there in the end, we always do. Unfortunately it's company policy never to return money."

Redrum walked purposefully towards him, removing a folded knife from his coat pocket as he did so. "I'm afraid your time's up, Goldman. I'm going to have to terminate your contract," he said, flicking open the knife's gleaming blade. He flipped the knife between his hands, juggled with it briefly and then lunged at Hymie.

BANG!

Redrum collapsed like a punctured balloon into a crumpled heap in the alleyway.

"Bloody hell!" cried Goldman, not quite sure whether to be more shocked by his own narrow escape or the fact that Mike, from the best of motives, had shot their client stone dead.

Mike slipped the shooter back into his jacket pocket and walked over to the body. The sound of running footsteps and a police siren from a neighbouring street made him stop momentarily.

"I didn't know you were carrying a gun," said Hymie.

"Well, after that night in the basement with the poison dwarves I haven't been sleeping so well. Besides, you're not complaining, surely?" said Mike, as he stooped down to reveal the face of their erstwhile client.

"Not much more than a kid," continued Mike. "Do you recognise him?"

"No," said Hymie, looking down at the body with difficulty.

"Me neither," said Mike, "but it was you or him, Hymie, and I wasn't going to stand by and watch you get creamed, even if you are a bloody useless detective."

All the fight seemed to have drained out of Goldman. "Let's get out of here, Mike, before the Fuzz arrive. And thanks, by the way."

"It's okay, mate. Where to now?" asked Mike.

"The medium, where else? We need an alibi as well as some answers," said Hymie, leading the way briskly along the road towards the nearest bus stop.

Aspbury Towers, Palmers Green was a slightly tired-looking Art Deco apartment complex which had seen better days. Sadly it had suffered from one too many urban redevelopment projects and was now cast into the shade behind the local *Save a Packet*.

"Look, Goldman, twenty five litres of mayonnaise for a fiver!" said Mike as they passed the store's front window.

"Yeah, but it probably tastes like shit," said Hymie, dismissively. "Here we are, Mike," he added a moment later, pressing the buzzer for apartment number 21.

A crackling intercom sounded out in the still night air.

"Who is it?" asked a female voice.

"I thought she was meant to be psychic," said Mike, smirking.

"Shhhh, don't be so rude," hissed Hymie. "Hello, is that Madame Za Za?"

"Yes, who is it?" she asked.

"Hymie Goldman, I called to arrange a meeting."

"Yes, I remember, something about a missing person. Did you come alone?"

"No, I'm with my business partner, Mike Murphy. Can we come in?"

There was a pregnant pause while Madame Za Za considered her options or phoned a friend, before the intercom crackled into life once more.

"Yes, alright, I'm on the third floor, number 38."

"I thought you were number 21" said Hymie.

"You can't be too careful in this business so I give out a false address to keep the nutters away," said Madame Za Za.

There was a buzzing sound and a click as the door catch was released and then Goldman and Murphy entered the building. They walked across the lobby to a small lift in the corner. Hymie groaned, removing the 'out of order' sign from the door and discarding it behind him.

"How am I supposed to climb three floors with *my* knees!" he snapped.

"Well, you could always call up Madame Za Za to give you a piggy back," said Mike.

"You think she'd go for that?" asked Hymie.

"No," said Mike.

They dragged themselves up three flights of stairs and along two landings before arriving breathless outside number 38.

Mike pressed the doorbell and the door opened on a security chain.

"Can I see some ID please?" asked the feeble voice proceeding from a bundle of shawls behind the door.

"Ah, yes, sure. What did you have in mind? Finchley Public Libraries or an old Oyster card?"

"Just something with a name and photo ID will do," said Madame Za Za.

Hymie proffered an old bus pass. The old lady took it from him and studied it for some time behind the door.

"You poor man, how you must have suffered," she said.

"I'll have you know that was taken a few years ago when I was fitter," said Hymie.

Mike laughed.

Madame Za Za removed the door chain and the two detectives followed her through a narrow reception room into the lounge. The décor was so outlandishly bright it could only have been designed by a colour-blind designer; an orange settee here, some purple curtains there and a garish patterned rug in the middle of the floor. In pride of place on the rug sat a large round table, covered in a black satin tablecloth. Madame Za Za herself was scarcely less eye-catching. The parts of her you could see that is; mainly her hands, which were smooth, brown and covered in rings, while her body and face were swathed in silken robes and crowned by an almost totally opaque veil. For all they knew it could have been anyone under there.

"Sit down Mr Goldman, Mr Murphy, I've been expecting you."

"Well, you would have, I made the appointment a couple of days ago," said Hymie.

"No, I meant before that, Mr Goldman. It was foretold to me many moons ago that two men fitting your description would come in search of enlightenment."

Mike raised his eyebrows. This was the kind of baloney he'd been expecting.

"How do we know you have the power?" asked Hymie, suspiciously.

"Why else would you be here?" asked Madame Za Za.

Mike glared at Goldman as though he were wondering the very same thing. He started to get up from his chair.

"No matter," said Madame Za Za dismissively. "If you don't even have the sense to listen, then why should I care? Why should I care that Hymie Goldman and Mike Murphy, detectives of 792A Finchley Road, North London have failed to find the whereabouts of a magician whose name begins with the letters A.H?"

Mike and Hymie gawped at each other in amazement and Mike sat back down.

"I see you were only testing me, gentlemen, but you need have no doubts about my gifts. I come from a long line of Romanys," said Madame Za Za.

She lifted the black satin cloth with a flourish to reveal the tools of her trade; a large crystal ball, a deck of cards and some chicken bones.

"Cross my palm with silver or, shall we say, fifty quid, and I'll begin," said the mystic lady.

Hymie coughed up with an effort of will, then had a pain in his wallet where fifty quid used to be.

Za Za passed her hands over the crystal ball, uttered an outlandish chant and appeared to enter a trance.

"I see you've been having a lot of trouble lately," she said.

"You never spoke a truer word, love," said Hymie.

"When *haven't* you been having a spot of bother, eh, Goldman?" said Mike.

"Please, Mr Murphy, your scepticism is interfering with my mystic aura."

"Sorry madam," said Mike.

"The future is an open book to me," continued Za Za. "It's true that there are many possible endings but only I can see what will be. Que sera, sera."

"Go on, go on," said Hymie, half expecting her to burst into song.

"Are you sure you want to know what the future holds?" asked Za Za in deadly earnest. "No one will think any the less of you if you're not brave enough to face it," she added. "I mean, there's no shame in being chicken, or, even if there is, at least you can sleep nights."

"Come on, Za Za, I've got fifty quid at stake here, what's going to happen to me?" asked Hymie.

"Very well; I see two men in uniform, standing over a body."

"Whose body?" asked Mike.

"I can't see his face, he's wearing a mask," said Za Za.

"How convenient," said Mike.

"I can see a large man, surrounded by midgets," continued Za Za. "They are tormenting him until he snaps."

Mike's face became deathly white. "What happens next?"

"I see a magician in a cloak, casting spells over some large rocks," she concluded.

"But what does it all mean?" asked Hymie, anxiously.

"I can't tell. The spirits only give us glimpses of the truth. It's up to each of us to make our own sense of those insights," explained Za Za.

"But there's so little to go on," said Hymie, irritably. "Can't you tell us more? Where's Harvey?"

"I'm afraid not, Mr Goldman, the crystal is clouding over again."

"Well, what about reading my tea leaves? Or what about those chicken bones on the table?" asked Hymie.

"Oh, they're just left over from my tea. I had Kentucky fried chicken tonight," said the spirit medium.

"You're sure there's nothing more you can tell us?" persisted Hymie.

Madame Za Za spread the deck of cards across the table before him.

"Pick one!" she snapped.

Goldman tapped the back of a card and Za Za picked it up and looked at it.

"To find Harvey you must first visit the pyramid, but beware Bolton."

They left the apartment in something of a daze, not sure whether they had been duped or given vital clues to the mystery that enveloped them.

As they walked down the staircase, Mike noticed an apartment with a broken down door and smoke streaming from the shattered windowpane. Ironically the number on the wall outside was 21.

As they opened the door onto the street they were met by a wall of headlamps. They were about to turn and run when a policeman with a megaphone hailed them.

"OK Goldman, Murphy, put your hands above your heads and lie face down on the pavement."

"I can't do both at the same time, I'm a sick man," protested Hymie.

"You do not have to say anything, but it may harm your defence if you do not mention when questioned something which you later rely on in court. Anything you do say may be given in evidence," said the policeman.

"You say the sweetest things, Terse," muttered Mike.

"The pleasure's all mine, guys," said the sergeant.

Part Eighteen

Musical Chairs

Click! Decca's finger depressed the record button on the interview room tape machine, leaving the rest of him free to depress his least favourite suspect.

"Interview with Hymie Goldman, 11.15 December 19th, Inspector Decca and Constable Potter in attendance," he said, curtly. Potter may as well have been taking a nap for all he was contributing.

"I'm no good at interviews," bleated Hymie. "I get all anxious, sweat breaks out along my hairline and I get a terrible itching in the small of my back," he added.

"All classic symptoms of a guilty conscience, Goldman," said Decca.

"I wouldn't know, Inspector. Still, are you sure you wouldn't rather send me a questionnaire through the post? Or if you don't trust the mail we could always exchange texts or have a facebook chat," wittered Hymie, nervous as hell.

Nothing any good ever came of being interviewed by the Fuzz, he thought.

"Ho, ho, you will have your little joke, eh, Goldman," said Decca, "but I don't want to be your web buddy, I'll settle for asking all my questions here and now at New Scotland Yard if it's all the same to you, or even if it isn't. Now, let's begin with the end of your sorry career, shall we? Or are you still labouring under the delusion that you and that escaped gorilla, Murphy, are private detectives?"

"End of my career, Inspector? I don't mean to disappoint you but you've been calling for that for some time without much success," said Hymie.

Decca frowned. "I've never denied your talent for chaos and destruction, Goldman. I'm surprised MI5 haven't put a counter-terrorism unit on your tail to study your technique."

"It'll be the cutbacks," said Hymie.

"Right, Goldman, let's not beat about the bush, we've been here before. All you need to know is that we've got you on CCTV leaving what was left of the Magic Triangle's HQ on the night it was bombed; that Terse and I can testify to seeing you leave a murder scene at the Novotel Hammersmith and that we have witness statements from earlier this evening identifying you as the murderer of a man in a cape."

"Not Batman, surely?" quipped Hymie, feeling unequal to the tidal wave of circumstantial evidence approaching him. "OK, Inspector, I realise it doesn't look too good for me, I'm no fool. I know you've got a list of unsolved cases you're just itching to pin on me, but you know as well as I do that with the right brief none of it would stick in a court of law."

"Do me a favour, Goldman, when could you ever afford decent briefs? You usually get the kind of nurks who can just about manage to get you a suspended sentence when you didn't do it; losers like yourself. Tell me everything you know and I may consider putting in a word for you," said Decca.

"Haven't you ever heard of client confidentiality?" asked Hymie.

"Yes, but I'm surprised that you have," replied the Inspector. "Wake up and smell the coffee, Goldman! It's over. You're facing life behind bars. At this point I'd usually say 'and a pretty boy like you may never sit down again' but we both know I'd be lying."

"I never knew you cared, Inspector," said Hymie.

"I don't, but you will when it's all over. Give me a reason not to stick you back in the cells, sunshine."

Hymie scratched the five o'clock shadow on his chin and tried to find a better solution than bloody-minded defiance.

"Look, Inspector, this case is just too big for JP Confidential," began Hymie.

"I thought no case was too large for you, Goldman?" smirked Decca. "At least that's what it says in your advertising."

"Don't get me wrong," said Hymie, defensively, "we'd get there in the end, we always do. We've got plenty of leads; naturally, it's just that we haven't cracked it yet. So, it occurred to me that if we pooled our resources we both might get a result that bit faster. Of course, for it to work you'll have to trust me. Can you do that, Inspector?"

Decca weighed him up non-commitally for a moment. "Tell me more," he said.

"My client was a gangland killer who wanted to know the whereabouts of a third rate magician called *The Amazing Harvey*," said Hymie.

"So he hires a third rate detective…I'm with you so far," said Decca.

It was Hymie's turn to look narked but he held his tongue.

"I couldn't find this Harvey character," he said. "He still seems to be lying low, what with all those magicians being killed and the Magic Triangle itself being attacked. Anyway, the client turned up this evening wanting his money back…"

"How inconvenient. So you shot him I suppose?" asked Decca.

"No, I'm a man of peace, Inspector. I'm not cut out for violence. If you must know, the client started threatening me with a knife when some complete stranger happened along and shot him. Thankfully it was a rough neighbourhood," said Hymie.

"How very convenient!" said Decca.

"Naturally I scarpered," concluded Hymie.

"Alright, Goldman, I can believe in you running away from a fight but tell me, what was the name of your client and can you describe the man who killed him?"

"I only knew him as Redrum," said Hymie. "I always assumed that was an alias."

"No kidding, Goldman. So you never twigged that in addition to being the most famous Grand National winner of all time it was also 'murder' spelt backwards?"

It looked like all those hours spent poring over the crossword had paid off, thought Decca. Hymie gaped. Was it just a coincidence or had Decca actually stumbled onto a clue that he'd missed? It didn't seem to mean much but it was enough to make him feel like a prize wally. He collected himself together. "Very clever, Decca, but what difference does that make to the price of pizza?"

"Describe this Redrum for me," continued the Inspector.

"I never saw his face, he always stayed on the other side of a cape whenever we met and he spoke with a strange accent," said Hymie.

"How strange? Walthamstow? Dagenham? Or was he from north of the Watford Gap?"

"He was a foreigner all right. I thought he might be from Russia," added Hymie.

"You mean the Kremlin?" asked Decca.

"I guess they could be in on it too."

"And who shot him?" probed Decca.

"It was too dark to see. Besides, I wasn't hanging around to find out, was I?" said Hymie.

"So it wasn't Mike Murphy then?" asked Decca.

"Good lord, no. Whatever gave you that idea?" asked Hymie. "Look, that's as far as I got, Inspector. My client's dead so I don't have a case any longer. Why don't you just save yourself the paperwork and let me go? Then if, in the fullness of time, I can be of any further assistance please don't hesitate to call. You'll be wasting your time though," he added, helpfully.

"Let me be the judge of that, Goldman. There's more going on here than meets the eye. Even if I were to accept your story, which I have to say, I don't, that still leaves the inconvenient facts of your presence at the bombed out Magic Triangle HQ and at the Novotel, Hammersmith on the night Marvo the Magnificent was murdered."

"I'd love to help you, Inspector, I really would, but these things are just coincidences. I was passing the Magic Triangle when it blew up so

I naturally tried to help find any survivors, and there must have been thousands of people walking through Hammersmith on the night that magician died. Anything else is just a conspiracy theory. I'm just a hardworking private investigator, not one of the four horsemen of the Apocalypse," said Hymie.

"But that's just where you're wrong," said Decca. "Death, Famine, Plague… and Hymie Goldman, what a lethal combination; you never said a truer word," he added, laughing. "Still, I don't have to sit here and listen to Jackanory when I've got a warrant to search your offices, do I?" said Decca, slapping the document down on the interview room table in front of him.

Goldman looked morosely from Decca to Potter and back again.

"You won't find anything there," he said. "I keep all my records up here," he added, tapping the side of his forehead with his right index finger.

"Well, I suppose it keeps the running costs down eh, Goldman? I mean, why go to the expense of a filing cabinet when you only have two files and a selection of final reminders?" asked Decca.

They'd finally succeeded in annoying him, thought Hymie; the arrogant Detective Inspector and his dumb stooge of a constable. Where did they get off taking the piss out of a hard working local businessman? His taxes paid their wages. Or, at least, they would have done if he'd paid any.

"OK, Decca," said Hymie, "so you want to know what gives with the Magic Triangle? Well, it'll cost you. I can blow open the whole damn case and see to it that you make Commander within the next couple of weeks but Murphy and I walk out of here today." He eyed them like a card sharp holding a pair of twos.

"Interview suspended at 11.45," said Decca, switching off the recording machine.

"You'd better not be bullshitting me, Goldman or you'll never work in this city again," said the Inspector.

"Promises, promises," replied Hymie, never an enthusiastic devotee of hard work.

"Come on then, Goldman what *have* you got for me?" asked Decca.

Hymie felt like a hedgehog caught in the approaching headlights of a truck. Now that it was finally time to put up or shut up he realised he'd already given away practically everything he knew. He could babble on about dwarves and parrots for a while but that would only get him locked up in a loony bin. How could he possibly invent something big enough to get Mike and himself out of there? He decided to play for time and on the Inspector's Achilles heel; his craving for promotion.

"Hold it, Decca. Before I give your career the boost it so desperately needs, what guarantee do I have that you'll let Mike and I go free? I mean, you could be swanking around on the twentieth floor with the keys to the executive bogs while we're languishing behind bars," said Hymie.

A wistful look played across the Inspector's careworn face.

"What information is it you're *actually* offering me?" he asked. "You've already told me you don't know the whereabouts of *The Amazing Harvey*, so what *do* you know, Goldman? Do you know who's behind the magician killings and where I can find them?"

It was Hymie's turn to look pensive. Oh, he could fabricate a ludicrous story with the best of them but would Decca believe it and even if he did, would he let them go or have it checked out first? The latter could be fatal to his prospects of early release.

A thunderous knocking on the interview room door was followed by the appearance of a crew-cut head in the doorway.

"Chief, I need a word urgently," it said.

"Now's not a good time, Terse," replied Decca.

"But it's *important*, sir," added the sergeant with conviction.

Decca stood up, collected his thoughts then strode purposefully out into the corridor, closing the door firmly shut behind him. He was about to give Terse a piece of his mind when he noticed a huddle of ne'er do wells further down the corridor and thought better of it. In the midst of them all stood Mike Murphy like a bouncy castle at a funeral, handcuffed and surrounded by constables. Behind him on the bench sat two city-types in pinstriped suits and red braces, clutching what appeared to be a brief.

"I'm afraid we have a habeas corpus problem on our hands, sir," said Terse, lowering his voice in a stage whisper.

Decca gaped at the sergeant. Latin proceeding from Terse's gob had to be one of the most improbable sounds he'd ever heard; about as likely as the Chief Constable farting on News at Ten.

"Eh?" said Decca.

"*Habeas corpus,* sir; it's a writ or legal action through which a prisoner can be released from unlawful detention," added Terse, brightly.

"I know what it is, Terse! I just didn't expect to hear it mentioned in a conversation with *you*. GBH, yes, latin, no. Besides, we've only just arrested them, how on earth can we have a habeas corpus problem?"

"Well, sir," continued the sergeant, lowering his voice still further. "It looks like the case is falling apart."

"How can that be, Terse?" asked Decca, sounding like a small boy who'd had his ice-cream nicked and sand kicked in his face for good measure. "This time we've got them bang to rights. We've got the body…"

"Er, sorry to be the bearer of bad news, Chief, but it seems that the body has walked out of the mortuary. The victim wasn't quite as dead as we thought," added Terse helpfully.

"That's the craziest thing I've ever heard!" groaned Decca in disbelief.

"It's worse than that, though," continued Terse.

"Worse? How on earth can it be worse, Terse?" snapped Decca.

"We can't find the weapon used to commit the crime," said Terse, as nonchalantly as he could manage.

"We *know* Murphy shot the guy, even if we don't have a body or a weapon, we can hold them on suspicion," said Decca in desperation.

"Sorry, sir," said Terse. "I did say it got worse. I've just had a call from DCI Donkin."

Decca closed his eyes and put his hand to his forehead. Whatever the sergeant was about to say scarcely mattered, it was well understood that no one argued with Donkin. "What did he say?" asked Decca.

"He said he'd had a call from Goldman's lawyers," said Terse, nodding in the direction of the two suits on the bench. "He said they were a couple of legal eagles from the city; Fothergill and Dungannon or someone, and we had to let them see their clients at once or we'd have to answer to him."

Decca shuddered. He'd sooner let the devil incarnate out onto the streets of London than answer to DCI Donkin. What he wouldn't give for something on the old dinosaur, like these city-types seemed to have.

"I don't believe it!" gasped Decca. "How the hell does Goldman do it?" he added, as his left eye began to twitch.

"Someone upstairs seems to like him, Chief," said Terse.

"But why?" snapped Decca. "OK, Sergeant, send in Fothergill and Dunmoanin. Presumably they'll want Murphy too?"

"That's what DCI Donkin said, sir."

"OK, what's the point in arguing, Terse? Before they go in let me just have a final word with Goldman. You never know, I may just be able to get a last piece of useful information out of the crafty sod, if he doesn't realise the party's over."

Decca re-entered the room and invited Potter to leave them.

"Good news, Inspector? Am I free to go?" asked Hymie

"Yeah, in some parallel universe perhaps," said Decca. "No, I thought I'd just check whether you had anything else to say before I returned you to the cells."

"I thought we had a deal, Inspector," said Hymie. "Putting me back in the cells wasn't part of it and the same goes for Murphy."

Decca stared across the desk at the battered man of fortune and grimaced.

"It's true what they say, Goldman, the devil looks after his own. Apparently your lawyers have arrived."

"I have *lawyers*?" replied Hymie, incredulously. "Hah, I mean, yes, of course, where have they been all this time? Oh, and they didn't happen to mention the name of the firm, I suppose?" Hymie's mind was racing. Who could these *lawyers* be and why did they want to see him? Could he play it to his advantage and get out of jail free or were they a couple of hit-men come to silence him for good?

"I'm sure you'll find out when you get their bill," said Decca. "They didn't look like your usual low budget outfit though. Still, if anyone ever needed good lawyers it was you and Murphy. I'll send them in," he added, as he left the interview room.

After a brief game of musical chairs, Hymie and Mike found themselves seated opposite two total strangers in smart suits.

"Allow me to introduce myself, Mr Goldman," said the senior of the two, a tall man of indeterminate age with dyed blonde hair. "I'm Fothergill and this is my colleague, Dungannon," he explained, indicating a pale youth with glasses who didn't look old enough to be a lawyer. "We're the men you've been waiting so long to meet," he added.

"Pleased to meet you," said Hymie, feeling slightly more confident that they weren't hit-men but still wondering what they were doing there.

"OK, H, who are these two nonces?" growled Mike, getting instantly to the nub of the matter.

"We're your *lawyers*," said Dungannon, as though trying to convince himself.

"We don't have lawyers," said Mike, "although I didn't realise we had accountants until recently so I could be wrong," he added.

"Well, I'm Fothergill and this is Dungannon," said the elder man, clutching his brief. "We're living proof that you *do* have lawyers."

"Wait, yes, I see now," said Mike. "Decca thinks we've finally flipped and he's stuck us in a room with these two other delusional nutters while he phones for the dial-a-bus to Broadmoor. We can all share a padded cell!"

"I knew this was madness," said Dungannon irritably to Fothergill.

Fothergill was clearly made of sterner stuff.

"We are where we are, Mr Goldman and Mr Murphy. Imagine, if you will, that you are both in a police interview room being observed through one way glass by a disgruntled police inspector and the two men sitting opposite you are your best chance of getting out of here."

"Yes, anything for a laugh, but who *are* you?" asked Hymie.

"Fothergill and Dungannon," repeated the elder man as though reciting a spell.

"I couldn't give a monkey's if they're Tom and Jerry if they really can get us out of here," said Mike.

"All you both need do is nod at everything I say for the next few minutes while my colleague here takes notes and you'll soon be walking out of here as free men," said the man known as Fothergill.

What was going on? wondered Hymie, nodding along to the imaginary conversation. They'd been hired to find a failed children's entertainer; a task that they'd failed, by a killer who they'd been forced to kill. Now they were trying to get out of a police station by pretending to answer questions for two men who were masquerading as their lawyers. They didn't look much like lawyers but then how would he know? They didn't have any lawyers. So who were these guys and what did they want? Everything seemed incoherent yet strangely connected. They'd failed to find *The Amazing Harvey* but what if he'd decided to come looking for them? Would he know where to begin? Hymie stared hard at Fothergill and Dungannon but they simply shook their heads at him like nodding dogs in a rear-view mirror and continued pretending to take notes.

"Our work here is done," said Fothergill, standing up at last.

"About bloody time," said Dungannon.

"You wouldn't know anyone called *The Amazing Harvey*, I suppose?" asked Hymie, trying to catch the legal eagles off guard.

"No, sorry," said Fothergill.

"Nor his assistant, Boltini," said Dungannon as the fake lawyers left the interview room, still clutching their unopened brief.

In the observation room next door, Decca and Terse looked on with dejected fascination.

"I suppose we'll have to let those two idiots out now, Terse," said Decca.

"Unless you want to be the one to tell DCI Donkin, sir," said Terse.

"Well, if that's the way it's gotta be then so be it, but I want *everyone* watching them, do you understand, Terse? Homicide, Narcotics, the Fraud Squad, the Transport Police, Meals on Wheels, Finchley Public Libraries; in fact anyone in a blue uniform with a big hat. I don't want that pair to be able to take a leak in this town without me knowing about it. We're gonna bug them so hard they'll suspect us of being in the room with them. Sooner or later they'll crack, just you wait and see."

"Yes, sir!" said Terse vehemently. This was the kind of policing he'd joined the force for; no nonsense, twenty-four seven harassment of delinquents and low lives, and they didn't live much lower than Hymie Goldman and Mike Murphy.

Part Nineteen

A Lambeth Walk

It was late in the evening by the time Hymie and Mike finally hit the pavement outside New Scotland Yard. Potter had needed the overtime so it had taken him even longer than usual to complete the paperwork. A host of passers-by flitted past in their own little worlds, oblivious to the two unsightly strangers.

"OK, H, let's just pack our bags and get away from here," said Mike. "Somewhere hot where the beer's cheap, the natives are friendly and there's no extradition treaty with the UK."

"What? We can't leave *now*, not now that things are finally starting to get interesting," replied Hymie.

"You're insane, Goldman! Come to that I must be too, to have worked with you for so long. I've grown accustomed to the bizarre challenges of our working lives, to the prospect of meeting new and interesting people on a daily basis and to the fact that most of them seem to want to kill me!" snapped Mike.

"Mike, Mike, you exaggerate. No one's tried to kill you in weeks. It's usually me they're after. Besides, I don't think we could avoid this case if we tried. Look up there," said Hymie, gesturing at the grim concrete facade of New Scotland Yard. Lights shone down upon them from a wide array of windows and a dozen blinds twitched as they walked on down the street.

"If Decca hasn't got us under close surveillance by now I'll eat my hat," added Hymie.

"I thought you'd eaten that on the last case," said Mike.

"It's just a figure of speech, Michael."

"So where *are* we going?" asked Mike resignedly.

"It's nearly Christmas, Mike, let's go and visit a massive Norwegian Spruce with some twinkling lights. Covent Garden's only a short trek away, let's check it out and get something to eat while we're there," said Hymie.

Mike's stomach rumbled in agreement. "Excellent idea, H," he said.

Meanwhile, across the great metropolis of London: in Lambeth the members of the local Rotary group had assembled in disguise as Santa and his elves for their annual Christmas charity collection. Eighteen normally law abiding citizens and upright members of the community leant around sipping mulled wine and freezing their costumed butts off while their transport co-ordinator, a part-time elf called Geoff Scrivens, made his final inspection of the float.

A sixty-foot trailer covered in fake snow with an MDF sleigh on top sat waiting at the kerbside, hooked up to their ancient Land Rover with the tragically poor suspension.

"Looks alright to me," said Geoff, dismissively. "Where's our designated driver? Has anyone seen Mr Patel?" A surge of Chinese whispers spread across the crowd like a Mexican wave; "Mr Patel? Mr K-Tel? Anyone seen Mr McTell?" before one of the group, Vicky Green, an elfette in sexy black stockings, suddenly remembered he'd phoned in sick.

"Sorry everyone, too much mulled wine I'm afraid." she said, giggling.

"You're kidding," said Geoff, "So we've got no designated driver and everyone's had a drink."

"Well it is Christmas, matey," said Tim Wotherspoon, who ran the local locksmiths.

"There must be someone who can drive this thing?" asked Geoff plaintively. "After all, think of all those kids we'll be letting down if Santa doesn't pay them a visit. Not to mention all the money lost to good causes," he added.

"It's terrible the way they commercialise Christmas these days," said Elsie Pickles, the local postmistress.

"I hope you're not referring to the Rotarians, Elsie, we do a lot of good work for charity you know," said Geoff, tetchily.

"No, I meant everyone *else*," replied Elsie quickly.

"We could ask the Nelsons' new au pair," said an elfette with a half-full glass of mulled wine who was resting against the Land Rover. "She's over there," she added, pointing vaguely heavenwards. "I think her name's Nookie."

There were a few laddish guffaws from the predominantly middle-aged men in the group before Geoff silenced them with a frown and a shushing noise. "Nookie!" he cried. More guffaws.

"I think you'll find her name's 'Nuka', like *nuclear*," said Sam Nelson, enunciating clearly so as not to slur his words.

A tall blonde girl of twenty one with dazzling cornflower-blue eyes approached them. Her command of English was slight but she had already discovered that in her case it scarcely mattered.

"Yes, I Nuka. Can help, yes?" asked the blonde bombshell.

"You drive car, yes?" asked Geoff Scrivens, reverting to pidgin English as he always did when faced with a foreigner.

"Yes, just like that!" said Nuka, clicking her fingers. It was one of her favourite English expressions, generally prompting a smile from whoever she used it on.

"Great, thanks, Nuka. You see we've all had a few too many and we need someone to drive the Land Rover," explained Geoff.

"Few is many? Drive? Yes, just like that!" she confirmed, cheerfully. How hard could it be? She'd been driving her father's tractor for years.

"Thank God for that," muttered Geoff under his breath, as he would recall later.

"Here are the keys," he added, handing them over to her, "I've programmed the satnav so you only have to follow the instructions. Just stick to ten miles per hour and take it easy around the bends and you'll be fine."

"Round the bend," repeated Nuka, smiling.

She looked at the keys in her hand, then at the smiling faces of the group and decided to go with the flow. After all, what had it said on the au pair agency's advertising poster? 'Travel abroad, meet new people, learn new skills', and why not?

"OK, everyone aboard the float who's meant to be!" cried Geoff. "Donation collectors grab a bucket and follow on behind."

"It's a float, not a ruddy cart-horse," quipped Terry Jones, a builder in a baggy Santa costume, as he struggled onto the back of the float. He was soon joined by half a dozen slightly inebriated elves and elvettes.

"When you're ready, Nuka," said Geoff merrily.

Nuka opened the door of the 1976 vintage Land Rover, settled herself into the driving seat and turned the key in the ignition.

VrroooMMM!!

Yes, just like that! thought Nuka, just like papa's tractor. She revved the ancient diesel engine again and lifted her foot off the clutch.

VrrrrrrrrooooOOOMMM!!!

Geoff Scrivens blanched beneath the rosy cheeks of his elf costume as the Land Rover lurched forward before thundering down the road, at thirty miles an hour, away from the small industrial estate which had hitherto been home to the trailer.

A gaggle of bucket-carrying elves looked on aghast as Nuka waved to them in the car's rear view mirror. "Now turn left" said the satnav, causing Nuka to swerve to the right as she looked perplexedly around inside the car. The float disappeared rapidly from view, weaving drunkenly in and out of the scant evening traffic with the screams of those fairy-folk still clinging on for dear life drowned out by the jolly sound of 'Jingle Bells' blaring out over the society's clapped-out PA system.

Having arrived at Covent Garden and finding no Christmas tree, with or without festive lights, Hymie and Mike had adjourned to the nearest dodgy looking pub, *The Marquess of Anglesey*. They sat stuffing themselves with mediocre food and quaffing overpriced beer for over an hour, while the flow of reason stagnated into monosyllabic grunts. Finally Hymie leant back, replete in his creaky chair.

"OK, Mike, I'd better level with you, I didn't drag us over here to see a Christmas tree after all," he said.

"No kidding, Goldman? Thank God for that," said Mike, "I thought all that time in Scotland Yard must've softened your brain. So what *are* we doing here?"

"I've been thinking over what Madame Za Za said."

"What, about the magician with the large rocks?" asked Mike.

"No, about having to visit the pyramid to find Harvey," said Hymie.

"Look, mate, I'm not going to Egypt for you or anybody. I'd come down with the Pharoah's revenge on the first night and spend the rest of the time in the bog," said Mike, determinedly.

"Mike, there are pyramids all over London if you did but know it. That's where I think Madame Za Za meant; London, not Egypt."

"Oh, right," said Mike, distractedly pulling on his left earlobe in relief. He fell silent then started tugging at his lower lip for a change. Frankly this case was becoming a bit of a bore.

"So, don't you want to know where I mean?" asked Hymie, disappointed. He was about to explain his theory, when the pub door flew open and a gang of Teddy boys barged in, wearing their garish signature attire of brightly coloured jackets, drainpipe trousers and brothel-creepers. Leading the charge was Vinny Cable, leader of the East End Teds; instantly recognisable by an unfeasibly large quiff suspended precariously above his forehead and noted for his legendary grasp of late twentieth century economics. He pulled a comb from his pocket and brandished it around his well-greased locks in a gesture of surly defiance.

"What you lookin' at!" he barked at a middle-aged couple quietly drinking at a corner table. They turned away and started edging towards the door.

The barman hastily attempted to clear away everything breakable from the counter as Cable approached him.

"Oi, Mush! What's this?" said Cable, lifting a large metal ice bucket from the bar and placing it upside down over the barman's head. Ice cubes and cold water spilled down the barman's jacket and onto the bar. "Can you hear me in there, granddad? Don't you know I'm allergic to ice buckets?!" cried the delinquent economist.

"Bloody fascists!" cried Mike.

"Blimey, look at the time, Mike, we'd better be leaving, eh? How about going on somewhere else for a nightcap?" asked Hymie.

"Sorry, H, I just can't do it," said Mike, standing up. He flexed his knuckles then clenched and unclenched his ham-like fists three times while the pub interior seemed to grow darker.

"Oi, you!" said Mike.

Cable turned to face him with a contemptuous sneer across his smug face.

"This is a *nice* pub," said Mike. Sometimes you had to bend the truth in order to start a fight.

The East End Teds dissolved in riotous laughter. They'd heard the *Marquess* called many things but a 'nice pub' wasn't one of them.

Hymie stood up in solidarity. "Gents, gents, my friend has a highly developed sense of humour as you can see, but he also has serious medical issues. Forgive us but we can't stay and chat, my friend has to attend Outpatients," he said with misguided bravado.

"Only too glad to help you on your way to A&E," snarled Cable, taking a swipe at Mike.

Murphy flinched, but only enough to get in close with his follow through punch, which sent Cable flying gracelessly across the room towards the now deserted bay window. He landed in a crumpled heap on the floor.

At that precise moment, Nuka and a diminished band of elves, still clinging onto the wreckage of Santa's float with grim determination, bowled along the Strand at forty miles per hour while Jona Lewie exhorted passers-by to 'stop the cavalry' from the last remaining speaker in active service. Presumably he was referring to the squadron of police cars trailing along in their wake with festive lights a-flashing. Demolishing a bicycle stand, a red phone booth and two lampposts, Santa ploughed on regardless into Wellington Street although Santa's alter-ego, Terry Jones, was too preoccupied to do much waving. Smoke was now pouring freely from the Land Rover's engine compartment but Nuka kept going in the misguided belief that she was 'doing her bit for chastity', whatever that meant.

Back in the pub, the East End Teds were thoughtfully rearranging the *Marquess's* features, while Hymie tried to find a table that was still the right way up to hide under and Mike swatted any Teddy boy crazy enough to get within thumping distance. Vinny Cable seemed to have recovered sufficiently from their previous encounter to be looking for a quiet word with Murphy and he picked up one of the few remaining chairs as a peace offering.

Outside on the street, Nuka's Barmy Army were just about to float past the *Marquess of Anglesey* when the satnav suddenly piped up "now turn right." She applied the brakes sharply, to little effect, and swerved left. As she did so, a nut on the Land Rover's front right wheel pinged off, bringing Santa's goodwill mission to Covent Garden to an abrupt halt. The battered old four-by-four mounted the pavement and smashed into the front of the pub, flattening Vinny Cable and hospitalising an elf. Nuka climbed out of the car unscathed. Land Rover, not tractor she thought.

A traumatized Santa was later spotted running screaming into the night with a couple of shell-shocked elves limping after him, while two dishevelled men fitting the descriptions of Goldman and Murphy could be seen legging it down Wellington Street away from the cacophony of police sirens proceeding from the *Marquess of Anglesey* pub.

Part Twenty

Cadillac Heights

Dawn arrived uninvited at 792A Finchley Road with the thundering of the corporation dustcart and the plaintive cries of the local wildlife, coughing and spluttering their way into a new day. Mike arose irritably thanks to the cumulative aches and pains of narrowly escaping from a collapsing pub and sleeping on a settee which was simply too short for his great hairy legs. He peeked through the yellowed blinds and froze. A broad grin spread across his craggy face.

"Hey, Goldman, look at this!" he cried.

Hymie, as usual for the time of day, was asleep and snoring.

"Zzzzzzzzzzzzzz."

"Stop the snoring and come and have a deco at this, mate!" said Mike, shaking the scruffy sleuth from his slumbers as he dozed in his favourite chair with his overcoat buttoned up to his chin.

"Eh, wassermarrer? Is there any more toast, love?" asked Hymie.

"Love? Who are you calling love, you twonk?" snapped Mike. "Look, Goldman, you've gotta come and have a look at this pile of motorised crap someone's left outside."

Hymie stood up, stretched then slumped back into his chair again like a lifeless blob. He shared ninety-nine percent of his DNA with a jellyfish and it showed.

"What time is it?" he asked, as an afterthought.

"Oh, I dunno, seven? Seven thirty?" said Mike, without looking at his watch.

"I rest my case," said Hymie, closing his eyes.

"That has to be the biggest piece of shit I ever saw on a pavement," said Mike. "Hah, now he's getting a parking ticket," he added gleefully. "Hah, hah, serves him right, the prat. Imagine the cheek of the guy; first he buys the biggest all-American rust-bucket he can find then he dumps it in *our* street. There should be a law against it. Maybe there is. I can't wait to see the guy's face when he realises that not only does he have the worst car for miles around but he's got a parking ticket to go with it! C'mon, H, take a look at this car, and I use the word loosely. It's two different colours. I bet it's two old bangers welded together; they'd never paint it like that otherwise. I bet they'll be towing it away soon and you'll have missed it."

At the thought he might be missing out on something good, Hymie slowly regained consciousness and stumbled over to the window.

"What are you on about, Mike? Who's towing what, eh?"

"Maybe it was a decent car in its day…" continued Mike, "maybe it was *two* decent cars, but now it's just a wreck."

Hymie finally looked out of the window. His mouth opened and closed spasmodically but no sound came out. Mike watched him, first in surprise, then out of curiosity and finally with a dawning sense of realisation.

"It's yours isn't it?" he asked at last. "You actually bought that piece of junk."

"Ours, Mike, ours, and she's a 1969 Fleetwood, by the way," said Hymie. "A genuine classic."

"So are you," added Mike. "A genuine classic, one hundred percent proof, idiot."

"Well, we needed a new company car and they said they could deliver in a hurry," said Hymie, looking for a bright side.

"I'll bet they did. They wouldn't want that eyesore cluttering up the forecourt for long," said Mike. "Probably had it on the back of the trailer the moment they'd got the dosh."

"Isn't she a beauty?" continued Hymie, regardless.

"I can think of a few good words for it, mate, but *beauty* isn't among 'em," said Mike. "More to the point, I thought we'd agreed there'd be no more big spend items without talking to me or the accountants first."

"What, Furball and Mildew?" asked Hymie.

"Yeah," said Mike.

"Oh, I made them up," said Hymie, quietly.

Mike ground the knuckles of his right fist into the palm of his left hand in annoyance. "I knew it. I *knew* you were lying, I mean, what kind of firm calls itself Furball and Mildew?"

"Exactly," said Hymie. "They'd have been rotten, even if they did exist." He gazed fixedly at their new wheels on the pavement below to forestall further conversation. "Look, Mike, do you want to stand here bickering while they tow away our vintage motor or shall we take her for a spin?"

"Well, when you put it like that," conceded Mike, "where are the keys?"

"They said they'd leave them behind the sun-visor," said Hymie.

They eyeballed each other in startled amazement momentarily before running at full tilt down the stairs and out onto the street.

"Well, no one's nicked it, it *must* be junk," said Mike.

Hymie just climbed into the driving seat and revved the V8 engine like a geriatric boy racer.

"Music to my ears!" he mused.

Mike climbed in, belted-up and they roared off down the Finchley Road with the CD player blaring out 'No More Heroes' by the Stranglers.

"Can't you switch that racket off?" asked Mike, half a mile later.

"Ah, no, sorry," said Hymie, "the CD's stuck inside."

Mike punched the display on the front of the player and the band sounded like they'd fallen off a cliff. At any rate the music died.

"You need to control your aggression better, Mike," said Hymie.

"What chance do I stand, working with you?" said Mike.

The road took them north through a dozen congested suburbs

until the car had nearly guzzled all their petrol and Goldman needed a leak. He pulled off the road into a lay-by and relieved himself in the bushes, thoughtfully left there for the purpose.

"So, why on earth did you buy this pile of junk, eh, Goldman?" asked Mike.

"Shhh, she'll hear you," replied Hymie. "Besides, I needed some wheels to pull the birds. I've been getting a bit lonely lately," he confided.

"I thought you'd given up on women," said Mike. "Let's face it, you've never had much success with them, have you, H?"

"Whereas you've been a right Casanova, you mean?" quipped Hymie. He didn't have to take abuse about not pulling birds from King Kong.

"I was only quoting you," said Mike. "I remember what you said after that last bird took you to the cleaners…Drearie? No, Deirdre. You said, 'Mike, if I ever look like I'm even thinking about chatting up another bird, stop me…whatever it takes, stop me.'"

"Yeah, well, I didn't mean it, did I?" said Hymie.

"You never do, mate," said Mike. "So who's the unlucky girl? Anyone I know?"

Hymie shuffled his feet. "Ruby," he said. "I was going to call Ruby and ask her out."

"What, the cleaner you hired who disappeared weeks ago with our petty cash?" said Mike.

"We don't know that, for sure," said Hymie. "She went out in search of cakes."

"Fair enough, H, with a mission that tough she could be back any day."

"So, I err…was wondering if you had her number?" asked Hymie.

"Well, yes, as it happens, it's on my mobile," said Mike, removing the handset from his jacket pocket and passing it over. "I can't wait to see your legendary bird-pulling technique in action, H," he added, smiling.

116

Goldman looked blankly at Mike then climbed out of the car and disappeared into the bushes again. He needed privacy if he was going to crash and burn over a woman again; Mike taking the piss would only make it hurt all the more.

Mike twiddled with the knob on the CD player, but the Stranglers had taken offence and weren't coming back. Only the sound of Goldman mumbling in the bushes gave him away. Finally he emerged smiling and returned the phone to Mike.

"Thanks, buddy," said Hymie.

"What did she say?" asked Mike.

"I'm seeing her tonight," said Hymie.

"Yeah, but what did she say?" repeated Mike.

"Well, I didn't actually talk to her but her auntie said she'd pass on the message and that Ruby would be sure to meet me tonight."

Mike smirked. "Yeah, and I'm the flying Dutchman."

Part Twenty-One

A Hot Date

Hymie sat at a small table inside *Hotcha Mocha* and stared regretfully into his full fat latte with chocolate sprinkles. It had cost him a tenner, but since he'd arrived an hour early for his hot date with Ruby and it was chucking it down outside, he didn't have a lot of choice.

Would she get his message? Would she bother to come? And what had happened to that twenty quid he gave her for cakes all those weeks ago? You could buy an awful lot of cakes for twenty quid. Or two coffees. He caught sight of himself in the café window and wondered if he would pass muster. He'd certainly taken more care than usual over his appearance; he'd showered, shaved, combed his hair and pressed his best suit overnight under the mattress. What more could any woman want?

"Excuse me, but is this seat taken?"

It wasn't Ruby but a tall thin man in a pinstriped suit with keen blue eyes, greying hair and a parrot on his shoulder. Hymie did a double-take. Ah, no, the parrot was on a poster of the Amazon rainforest on the wall behind him.

"It's a free country," said Hymie sarcastically, his ten pound cup of coffee weighing heavily on his mind. It seemed a bit much that in an empty café these wandering loonies still singled him out.

The man placed his cup on the table top and sat down opposite him. Close up he looked more like a fugitive merchant banker than an escaped nutter, but you could never tell.

Hymie looked intently at the stranger, who smiled back.

"Do I know you?" Hymie asked.

"No, but please let me introduce myself," said the stranger in a mid-Western accent, producing a business card from his inside jacket pocket. "My name's Lafarge, Cranston Lafarge the third."

"Is it some kind of hereditary title then?" asked Hymie, "or are there two others?"

"Oh, no, it's just a family tradition, you know. I represent the Farmer's Union Collective Insurance corporation of Texas."

"FUCIT?" asked Hymie.

"Pardon?" said Lafarge.

"I'm sorry, I never buy insurance in cafés," said Hymie. "Or anywhere else, come to that. I'm just not the insuring type," he added.

"What, nothing's ever gone wrong in your life?" asked Cranston.

"Oh, all the time," sighed Hymie, "I'm just too skint to buy insurance," he confided. That usually did the trick, but not on this occasion.

"Please, Mr Goldman, don't trouble. I'm nothing if not well informed and even if I were a gambling man, there are few people I'd be less likely to insure than you."

Hymie felt strangely insulted. Where did this guy get off? Coming in here refusing him life insurance; why, he could get comprehensive cover anytime, anywhere, no questions asked. He was about to give the guy a piece of his mind when it dawned on him that he didn't even want the blasted insurance.

"So, how do you know my name and how did you know where to find me?" asked Hymie, suspiciously.

"I made it my business to find out, Mr Goldman. You see, I have a serious proposition for you."

Hymie reflected on the last time he'd had professional dealings with an insurance company and shuddered. It had been an elaborate set up by an organised crime syndicate which had nearly killed him. He'd need to be mad to get involved with another insurance company.

"So, how much are you paying?" he asked.

"Don't you want to know more about the investigation?" asked Lafarge, surprised.

"What, with coffee at ten quid a cup?" replied Hymie, eyeing up the baristas bitterly. "I need every pound I can get."

"Well, I can assure you, sir, if you can deliver on your reputation, there's a big cheque waiting for you at the end of it," said Cranston.

Hymie flinched. Had this poor fool confused him with someone else? Or had he, Hymie 'Megabucks' Goldman suddenly acquired a reputation for something that attracted big money? And while he was asking big questions, why was his life becoming so random?

"Well, Mr Cranston the third, what can I do for you?" he asked.

Lafarge leaned forward in his chair and lowered his voice. "We want you to recover a certain device from the Red Square," he said.

Hymie weighed up the suited wonder for several seconds. No, there was no other explanation, he was plain nuts. He wondered briefly which high security establishment he'd escaped from and then decided to play along for laughs.

"What kind of device are we talking about?" asked Hymie.

"A Quark bomb," replied Lafarge.

"I've never heard of it," admitted Hymie.

"I'm not surprised," conceded Lafarge. "Let me fill you in. You know, I presume, that the Red Square is in the employ of the Millennium Group?"

"What, the hotels and conferences group?" asked Hymie.

"Hah, very good, Goldman, no, the group of religious fanatics and anarchists based in Wacko, Texas," said Lafarge. "They have been planning an 'end of the world' party for some time now and, unlike some other groups of crazed madmen who confine themselves to forecasting the date of Armageddon, have sufficient resources to make it really happen. The Quark bomb has long been rumoured theoretically possible, but now we believe it may actually exist."

"And what can it do, this Quark bomb?" asked Hymie out of morbid curiosity.

"Only suck the earth into a black hole."

"Pretty bad, then," said Hymie.

"The end of life, the universe, everything as we know it," confirmed Lafarge.

"And you want *me* to get this bomb away from Red Square?" asked Hymie, incredulously.

"Not Red Square, *the* Red Square; the terror organisation who have been trying to kill the magician you're investigating."

"*The Amazing Harvey?*"

"Exactly."

"I see," said Hymie, wondering why he hadn't stuck to lost pet investigations. "So what's Harvey got to do with it?" he asked.

"He's just a fly in the ointment," said Cranston.

Poor devil, thought Hymie. The world's gone mad and a bunch of terrorist nutters are out there trying to kill a harmless magician.

"Is there anything else I should know?" asked Hymie.

"Only that the Millennium Group has forecast the end of the world in forty-eight hours, so you haven't much time to find the bomb," said Cranston.

Hymie looked around the café for the hidden camera but it didn't seem to be there.

"So, the world's about to end and I'm the only person trying to stop it?" asked Hymie, jovially.

"No, of course not," said Lafarge. "We've got the FBI, CIA, MI5, 6 and 7, and every other intelligence organisation in the world looking into it. It's just that we've been getting a bit desperate," he conceded.

The be-suited wonder passed an envelope across the table to Goldman. "They asked me to give you this," he said simply.

Hymie opened it and removed what appeared to be a blank cheque.

"It's signed and dated," said Lafarge, "but the amount's blank. If you can find the bomb and return it to me within the next forty-eight hours, you can put any number you like in the box. If not, it probably won't matter."

Hymie had been about to make his excuses and head off for his hot date at the Freemont cinema, but now that the world was about to end it suddenly seemed embarrassing to admit it.

"Consider this my top priority," he said.

"Thank you, Mr Goldman," said Cranston Lafarge, holding out his hand.

Hymie shook it vigorously.

"And may the hopes of the world be with you," added Lafarge earnestly. He stood up and walked off into the night, leaving Hymie to finish the last few gulps of his ludicrously overpriced coffee.

Nah, just some nutter, he thought, as he drained his cup to the dregs. I wonder where he got the joke cheque from and who put him up to it?

Checking his watch, Hymie discovered to his horror that the film was due to start in five minutes so he hastily scattered a few old coins onto the tabletop and ran off in the direction of the Freemont.

Once inside the lobby, hot and dishevelled and with his date nowhere to be seen, he flattened down his hair and straightened his tie. Ruby was the kind of girl you often dreamt about but rarely met, and when you did you could never find the courage to ask out. He wondered again if she'd received his invitation and whether she would come. After all, he was scarcely love's young dream.

It was just as he was on the point of giving up hope that she arrived, breezily pushing through the revolving door and giving him an encouraging peck on the cheek.

"Hello Hymie, I nearly didn't make it," she said.

"I'm glad you did, Ruby," he replied, blushing.

"Well, I thought I owed you an explanation," said Ruby.

"It can keep," said Hymie, smiling.

"So, what are we seeing?" she asked.

"*This Gun for Hire,*" he said. "The classic film noir, c'mon or we'll miss the start."

He paid for the tickets and a large bucket of popcorn and they made their way silently up the stairs that lead to the auditorium.

Inside the theatre everything was pitch black but the movie had already begun so they found their seats by the flickering images on the screen. They shuffled along the back row in the half-empty theatre and took their seats together. Hymie had grown up watching vintage detective movies and they still held a fascination for him. He sat riveted to the screen as Veronica Lake began her familiar song and dance routine.

"I've got you and I'm enjoying it fine," she sang.

"I love this scene," said Hymie, his eyes transfixed on the film.

"I've got you right where I wanted you," sang Veronica.

"I'm over here, Hymie Goldman," whispered Ruby.

He turned to face her and she startled him with a passionate kiss fully on the lips. The bucket of popcorn fell unnoticed from his hands, disgorging its starchy contents across a wide area of the theatre floor. Suddenly the film he had loved for so long seemed to fade into the background as he gave himself up to the warmth of her embrace. Time stood still then raced ahead and left him gasping for breath, and all the thousand clues and blind alleys of this and every other case he'd ever worked on drained from him and left him feeling as light as a feather.

Part Twenty-Two

Home, home and deranged

In the penthouse suite of a skyscraper in downtown Dallas, Tex Avery, oil billionaire, evangelist and owner of the world's largest collection of cartoons, held court as Chairman of the Millennium Group. The Board meeting was attended, as usual, by an assemblage of sycophants and yes-men, recruited for their ability to agree to any ludicrous statement Tex cared to make, without so much as a murmur.

"Laydees and gentlemen, the day of our deliverance approaches," said Tex, chewing on a cigar the size of a small baguette. "In forty-eight hours a cute liddle Quark bomb called *Daisy-Belle* is gonna suck this planet into a black hole twice the size of Texas and those unbelievers are gonna look like a bunch of damn jackasses," he continued. "Boy would I like ter see Walt Disney's face when he realises he's been stuck in a freezer like a packet of frozen peas fer nuthin' this past fifty years!" cried Tex, with fervent glee.

He looked around the room to make sure all the dogs were nodding and smiled contentedly to find that they were.

"Yeah, and those scum-suckin' losers in the Davidian Cult of the Seventh Coming are gonna be kicking each others' butts to kingdom come when we get the date right for the end of the world, after they've been gittin' it wrong fer years!" added Tex, graciously. "The Mayans got it wrong, the Egyptians got it wrong and *they* got it wrong but Papa Tex, he knows!"

"Halelujah, Papa Tex!" cried Sybil Cronk, Head of Marketing.

"Amen, oh Great One!" cried Forrest Hawks, Head of Resources.

"Praise the Lord!" exclaimed Verne Crapowski, Head of Stationery.

Tex gazed expectantly around the room for further rapturous applause until his eyes alighted on Dave Clarke, Head of Accounting and Finance, who was busily tapping away on his pocket calculator. Dave stopped and looked up momentarily.

"Oh, that is good news," he said. Dave, who was British, had always struggled to overcome his natural reticence, even for a fat pay-cheque. Truth be told, he'd faked the whole evangelist thing just to get a decent job in a strange and alien country.

"How are we doing fer subscriptions, Dave?" asked Tex. Surely even a Limey bean-counter could be relied on to count to ten billion.

"Still coming in nicely thanks, Tex," said Dave.

Tex pulled the cigar out of his mouth and blew a large mushroom-cloud shaped smoke ring over his head.

"You betcha goddamned ass, Dave," said Tex. "We've gotta pay fer that darned Quark bomb somehow and I don't see why I should have ter pay fer it after all I've done for this organisation."

What had he done? wondered Dave. Only made an absolute fortune out of oil, gone round the bend and decided to blow up the planet to satisfy some demented form of megalomania. Someone had to stop the guy before it was too late. He looked around the room for support but they were all clearly deranged or high on narcotics. It had been all too easy to just keep taking the money and hope the madman would prove delusional but now the doubts were beginning to set in. What if he really had a *quack* bomb, whatever that was?

"Any questions?" asked Tex.

This was Dave's chance to stand up and be counted. He shuffled in his seat and stuck his hand in the air.

Tex looked at him in surprise like a teacher getting a question from the remedial kid at the back of the class.

"Where exactly is this Quack bomb?" asked Dave.

"Quark," corrected Tex. "Our agents in the UK have built it for

125

us," said Tex. "When I give the word, they'll press the button and poof! Game over," he added.

With British engineering there was hope for them yet, thought Dave.

"But, aren't they members of the Millennium Group themselves?" asked Dave. "Because, if not, how do we know they'll set off a bomb that will destroy themselves as well as all life on the rest of the planet?"

"Why, we have back-up, of course, Dave," said Tex, "we weren't born yesterday. We've hired a guy called Square, Red Square, he's an expert in his field."

Tex fixed him with a steely glare to forestall any further questions.

"Thank you, laydees and gentlemen. Now, if we've all finished, please join me in our communal prayer."

They all closed their eyes while Tex recited some dreadful bilge about the birds and the bees, parrots squawking in the trees and a large impending explosion putting an end to all living things on the planet. Dave made a mental note to get a proper job while he still could and the Board members all filed out of the room to attend other pointless meetings with other sycophants.

Part Twenty-Three

The Sound of Distant Thunder

Outside 792A Finchley Road it was snowing; big fat soft snowflakes that muffled the sound of your footsteps and blanketed everything in a dazzling layer of brilliant white. Mike sat inside, shivering on the tiny leather-effect sofa as their ancient central heating system had chosen that precise moment to pack up. It was almost as if, like Hymie, it had planned to down tools just as the real work was beginning.

Mike could have sworn he'd heard the rumble of distant thunder; either that or his stomach was playing up again. And where was that bum, Goldman? On the morning of December 21st he was nowhere to be seen. Not that he needed him, heaven forbid, but where else could he be? Despite his endless complaints on the subject, Hymie habitually slept in his office chair; it was as much a part of him as the five o'clock shadow and the fast food stains down his shirt.

There was a loud knocking at the door downstairs. Mike edged over to the window to see who it was, but the windows were all steamed up.

Carol singers? Jehovah's Witnesses? Who else would be daft enough to come calling in a snowstorm? wondered Mike. Of course, it could be Hymie, having left his car in a snowdrift and having lost his key.

"Coming!" shouted Mike as he lumbered down the stairs. He opened the door and looked out into the street. There on the step were two men in snow-covered coats like a couple of door-to-door snowmen.

"Did we call at a bad time?" asked the taller of the two, brushing the snow from his dyed blonde hair while his colleague attempted to de-frost his glasses.

"It depends what you came for," said Mike, cagily. "You see, I was thinking it was about time I started putting up my Christmas decorations so if you came here to try and sell me something or collect the payments on Goldman's car, I should beat it now, while you still have your teeth."

"Don't you remember us?" asked the man with frozen specs, anxiously.

Mike took a long hard look at the pair of them and then a faint glimmer of recognition dawned.

"You're those flamin' lawyers…Mildew and Muldoon. You haven't come for the money, have you?" asked Mike, suspiciously.

"No," said the taller man. "That's to say, we haven't come for the money and we aren't in fact lawyers but a couple of magicians."

"No kiddin," said Mike. "We've been looking for a magician, called…"

"*The Amazing Harvey*," said the taller man, holding out his hand.

"And Boltini," said the man with the glasses.

"Yeah, that's it," said Mike, "know where we can find 'em?"

"Sorry, Mr Murphy, *we're* Harvey and Boltini," explained Harvey.

"Oh, I see," said Mike, who, after searching half of London couldn't quite believe that they'd just turned up on his doorstep.

"If you'll let us in for a minute we can explain everything," said Harvey.

"Goldman's not here at the moment," said Mike.

"It's a matter of the utmost urgency, I assure you," added Boltini.

"Well, I was gonna put my feet up with a beer in front of the telly, see. It is Christmas, after all," said Mike, hesitantly.

"My dear Murphy, time is running out. If we don't speak to you now there may be no Christmas for you or anyone else, not this year nor any other," said Harvey, emphatically.

"Well, I suppose you'd better come in then," said Mike, reluctantly.

They re-assembled upstairs in the office and the two magicians shook the snow off their coats while Mike boiled the kettle.

"Help yourselves to a seat," he said, over his shoulder.

Mike passed out some mugs of tea and took up residence in Hymie's chair.

"So, what's this all about?" he asked.

"It's a long story and we don't have much time," said Harvey, "so stop me if I'm not making any sense."

"Oh, I'm used to it," said Mike, "I work with Hymie Goldman."

"As I understand it, Mr Murphy, you were hired by Redrum to find me," said Harvey.

"Yeah, but it doesn't matter any more," said Mike. "He's dead, I shot him myself."

Harvey smiled. "I'm sure you did, Mr Murphy, but he's not *dead*."

"Sure he is," said Mike. "I saw him lying there on the pavement, not much more than a kid."

"Redrum is a master of the dark arts, Mr Murphy. I've seen him jump from a burning building and fight off a small army of assassins without sustaining so much as a scratch," explained Harvey. "Whoever you saw lying on the pavement wasn't him. Or if it was, he wasn't dead but simply deceiving you with a skilful deception."

"Impossible," said Mike.

"Did you take his pulse or inspect his wounds?" asked Harvey.

"Well, no. There wasn't time," said Mike.

"That's all the opportunity he would have needed," said Harvey.

Mike felt confused. On the one hand it was a relief that he hadn't actually killed the guy but on the other, he couldn't quite believe it was true.

"So, where's Redrum now? And what's he up to?" asked Mike.

"He's trying to wipe out the Magic Triangle," said Boltini.

"Well he's not doing too badly so far," said Mike. "I was nearly killed in that explosion at the Magic Triangle's HQ in Euston. Are you saying that he was behind it?"

"Almost certainly," said Harvey.

"And is he working alone?" asked Mike.

"Almost certainly not," said Boltini. "He's one of the leaders of a terror organisation called the Red Square."

Mike sipped at his tea. "This isn't a wind up is it?" he asked, "only I've had enough wind ups to last a lifetime."

Harvey assured him that it wasn't.

"The Red Square and the Magic Triangle are sworn enemies," explained Harvey. "It was believed that the Square had been eradicated in 1938 when their last leader, Dan McGrew, was hung for murder, but somehow they've come back from the dead and they're intent on revenge. Someone must be funding them, we don't know who, but it's clearly some evil madman with deep pockets as they're rumoured to have dozens of new agents and some kind of atomic bomb."

"Great," said Mike, "just in time for Christmas. So what are *you two* doing about it?" he asked, taking a leaf out of Goldman's book on how to pass the buck.

"It's funny you should ask," said Harvey.

"Oh, hilarious," agreed Mike.

"Because that's why we came to see you. You see, the Square won't rest until every last member of the Triangle is dead and when they achieve that they'll come back and tie up the loose ends," explained Harvey.

"Like Hymie and me?" asked Mike.

"Precisely," agreed Harvey.

"So we may as well join forces now as wait for a knock on the door or an A-bomb through the letterbox later," said Mike.

"I couldn't have put it better myself," said Harvey.

"One thing I don't get," said Mike, "is how you, not being rude but, a *crap* magician, should know so much about what's going on. How is that?"

"It's a fair question, Mr Murphy," said Harvey.

"Yeah, so what's the answer?" asked Mike.

"Because I'm not nearly so bad a magician as I appear, my friend," said Harvey. "In fact I have the honour to be one of the sleeping dragons of the Magic Triangle. There are only a handful of us and we spend most of our careers..."

"Sleeping?" wondered Mike. It sounded like a good job for Hymie, he thought.

"In a way, yes; living on the very edge of normal society..." Definitely one for Hymie, thought Mike.

"Watching and waiting for the re-emergence of dark magic with all its attendant evils," concluded Harvey.

Mike took another sip of his tea, which had now gone cold. "You don't say," he said.

"I thought as much," said Boltini, standing up and removing an ugly-looking revolver from his jacket pocket. He pointed it at Harvey who instinctively started backing away.

"Stay where you are, both of you," snapped Boltini. "This little charade has gone on long enough. You see, I'm not the pathetic magician's assistant you think I am but a senior member of the Red Square. I've been working undercover as Boltini since Harvey's last assistant disappeared but now the hour of reckoning is upon us, or rather you. Tonight heralds the arrival of the winter solstice and we're planning a farewell party for the Magic Triangle at Stonehenge. All the missing magicians will be there, and you're both invited, naturally."

"I thought there was something funny about you," said Harvey, looking down his nose with disdain at his former assistant. "Just something sinister behind the specs."

"Is this a private argument or can anyone join in?" asked Mike. "After all, it is my gaff." He stood up and started to walk over to the window.

"I said stay where you are, Murphy, or I'll shoot," barked Boltini.

"What and alert the police?" asked Harvey. "Just take a look outside, Boltini, there are police surveillance men everywhere. Didn't you notice the green florist's van or the Mr Sloppy ice-cream van with no ice-cream or the team of road-menders around the corner? When did you last see a real road-mender out in the snow, eh?" he added.

"Or at all," said Mike.

Boltini walked over to the window. It seemed to be true, at least they were all out there, but could it just be another illusion? "Nice try, Harvey, but no coconut," he said. "Now sit down while I tie you up."

"I've had better offers," said Mike, starting to walk back to the settee.

Suddenly, there was a curious scratching noise at the window from behind them as Bacon made a bid to come in from the cold. Boltini turned instinctively towards the sound and Mike, seizing his chance, leapt across the room at him, knocking the gun to the floor. In the tussle that followed, Mike's size and strength quickly gained him the upper hand and as Boltini desperately reached out to retrieve his revolver, Mike knocked him cold with a well-aimed upper cut.

"Bravo, Mike!" cried Harvey.

Mike shrugged. "So, what shall we do with him?" he said, pointing at the crumpled figure of Boltini. "Were you serious about the police surveillance boys being outside?" he asked.

"Well, I can't say that they are and I can't say that they aren't," replied Harvey, "but it's probably best to leave first and then tip them off about the break-in later."

"Break-in?" asked Mike.

"Well, what else was he doing here?" asked Harvey.

"True, true," said Mike. "I'd better make sure the only prints on the gun are his," he added, as he retrieved the revolver from the floor with his handkerchief.

Part Twenty-Four

Under surveillance

The whole point of surveillance is to watch someone closely without being detected. In this way you gather reliable intelligence and can make informed decisions. Too much intelligence, however, and you can't see the wood for the trees. This is how it seemed to Inspector Ray Decca as he sat at his desk trying to sift through the huge pile of dead trees generated by his 'Get Goldman' campaign. In mobilising the mighty police surveillance machine for this purpose, he'd inadvertently brought Goldman and Murphy to the attention of those within the intelligence community who'd previously never heard of them, nor ever wanted to. Like Chinese whispers the story had spread, grown like wildfire and morphed into something beyond extraordinary; the Russian Secret Service believed Goldman to be an Israeli Special Agent with superhuman strength, the CIA, NSA and a host of other American acronyms believed him to possess incalculable psychic powers and the Chinese now ranked him as the fourteenth most dangerous man on the planet.

It would have amused and dismayed Decca to learn this, as he still had Goldman's card marked as an idiotic and persistent pain in the neck.

Terse burst into the room deep in the bowels of New Scotland Yard, brandishing his files.

"Do you wanna hear the latest on Goldman, Chief?"

Decca placed the last piece of his prawn mayo sandwich into his mouth, chewed it briefly and swigged his tea.

"Only if it's going to help us convict him," he said.

"Convict him of what, sir?" asked Terse.

"Anything will do," said Decca. "Preferably all the unsolved crimes on the books, given the amount of time and money we've spent watching him!" he added.

"Well, I've been working twenty-four seven, as you know, sir," said Terse, yawning. "And most of the other lads on the team haven't been home in days."

"Yeah, I've seen their takeaway expenses," said Decca. "I'd be surprised they had time to do any surveillance the amount of food they've put away. So, what's the latest, Terse?"

"Well, Chief, we tapped his phone but it looks like he only receives incoming calls and there were precious few of them. We also encountered some radio-wave interference on the remote receivers from that dodgy taxi firm around the corner, Ram-A-Jam Taxis."

"Yeah, I've heard their adverts on the local radio, they claim to be the cheapest cab firm for miles because they only use cheap crappy taxis. Why that would induce anyone to use them I can't imagine. Most of their cabs have been built from spare parts salvaged from insurance write-offs," said Decca.

"Shall I shut them down, Chief?" asked Terse.

"Go for it, Terse," said Decca. "Treat yourself. What else has been happening?"

"We've had 792B Finchley Road wired for sound for weeks now sir, but there's nothing to report," replied the sergeant.

"Probably because Goldman's office is at 792A, Terse," groaned Decca.

"Oh, yes, sorry, sir, I meant 792A," said Terse, although he clearly had his doubts.

"What about the rest of the cast of thousands working on the case? What have they come up with between takeaways, Terse?"

"Plenty, Chief," said Terse. "Constables O'Keefe, O'Toole, and Reidy are stationed at the back of the premises, disguised as road repairmen."

"Disguised, Terse?"

"Yes, sir," explained the sergeant. "They're wearing grubby boiler-suits, hard hats and haven't shaved for forty-eight hours. They haven't seen anything of Goldman, but O'Keefe's most insistent that there's a dangerous pothole that needs fixing."

"I don't believe it," said Decca.

"No, it was a genuine pothole, sir, he sent in some photos," said Terse.

"So, is that all we've got to show for hours and hours of overtime and a pile of paperwork, Terse? There's a dangerous pothole just off the Finchley Road?

"Ah, no, sir, I was forgetting constables Jones and Jackson. They took up position in the apartment opposite 792A Finchley Road with the thermal imaging camera," said Terse.

"Yes, and? Anything *hot* to report?" asked Decca, with a smirk.

"Well, apparently Mike Murphy spent twenty-five minutes in the loo, sir."

Decca shook his head in disbelief. "What about the eye in the sky?" he said. "Surely they've come up with something?"

"You mean the lads in the chopper, sir? Yeah, apparently they followed Goldman driving his new car for a couple of miles up the Finchley Road and then had to leave pronto to deal with a burglary in progress in NW3," said Terse.

"Oh, he's got a new car, has he?" asked Decca. "Ferrari? Porsche? Citroen 2CV?"

"No, some hideously deformed heap of American junk that looks like two old shoeboxes stuck together," said Terse, who had no soul when it came to cars.

"Discreet and understated like the man we know and loathe," said Decca.

Terse smiled and nodded.

"So, to sum it all up," said the Inspector, morosely, "after spending the entire departmental surveillance budget for the next three years, all we can say for sure is that Mike Murphy's had a dodgy curry and

Hymie Goldman's still got appalling taste in cars! They're going to kill me, you know that Terse, don't you," concluded Decca.

Terse observed a respectful silence at the imminent demise of Decca's career.

"Anything else I can do, Chief?" he asked.

"Well, Terse, I know Goldman of old," said Decca. "Something big's going down and I don't mean down Mike Murphy's toilet. Now's not the time to retire injured from the chase. Hit them with everything you've got; an extra man, tracker dogs, the Police and Criminal Evidence Act, tear gas, anything. I can probably get the overtime approved on the nod for a few days longer. We may as well be hung for a sheep as for a lamb, eh, sergeant?"

"Er, yeah," said Barry Terse, wondering what the Chief was wittering on about.

Part Twenty-Five

Ram-A-Jam ding dong.

There are businesses in London that could only exist in London because they couldn't get away with it anywhere else. They provide services below the radar of official recognition; so shoddy, cheap and nasty that their clients assume they must be getting a bargain. Ram-A-Jam Taxis was just such a business and given their commitment to the cheapest possible fares using the cheapest possible vehicles, their customers were literally taking their lives in their hands by getting into the back of one of their cabs.

The proprietor and general manager, one Mehmet Demirok, was a Turkish immigrant who'd pursued the dream of UK citizenship back in the nineties, circumventing the government's 'Look, no borders!' policy on the basis that it seemed too good to be true, by marrying a mentally unstable girl from Manchester. It had never been a love match, the relationship had gone horribly wrong almost immediately and he'd loathed Manchester, with its perpetual rain and grey skies, even more than his new wife. Undeterred and unafraid of hard work, he'd set off late one night with a suitcase full of readies to make a better life for himself in the metropolis. Ram-A-Jam Taxis had been the result.

Despite all Mehmet's hard work, Ram-A-Jam Taxis was a zombie firm; living proof that you did actually need to know something about the business you were in if you ever expected to succeed. If they broke one regulation concerning the commercial conveyance of passengers in a taxi or private hire vehicle, they probably broke the lot. However, it was their creative use of a proscribed radio frequency to transmit messages between base and their drivers which finally put them on a collision course with Sergeant Terse of the Metropolitan Police. They'd buggered up his surveillance operation and made him look a complete berk in front of the Chief and they were about to learn that some kinds of crime didn't pay.

On the morning in question the deputy controller, Larry Martin, sat hunched over his clapped-out console dishing out assignments to the great unwashed on their cash-in-hand payroll. "Pico, can you pick up Mrs Goodbody at 1 Bryanston Mews West, Marylebone," said Larry over the transmitter.

"Roger and out," came the prompt reply.

Pico Villalba, a Venezuelan, held the record for the most jobs completed in a single day; ninety-eight, although it was rumoured that he'd been high on coke at the time and that thirty-six of the jobs related to the same little old lady whom Pico had refused to let out of the cab. Most of the drivers were desperate, unhinged or on the run. Pico was all three.

"No show, Larry," came a distant voice from the ether. It was new driver Tommy MacDonald, who they'd taken to calling Ronald or Ron for short.

"I waited outside the Fat-Busters meeting for ten minutes but when I asked inside at the desk they got quite shirty," said Ron.

"What was the client's name, Ron?" asked Larry.

"Mr Jarse," replied Ron, "Hugh Jarse."

During the course of his first month the poor sap had been sent to a massage parlour to collect Norma Stitz, to a cosmetic surgery clinic looking for Ivor Biggun and now to a diet club in search of Hugh Jarse.

"You've fallen for it again, haven't you, Ron?" smirked Larry. "You're a hopeless case, mate. Just go and sit outside Kings Cross station till it wears off. You never know, you might strike it lucky," he added, laughing.

"Right-o," said Ron, "over and out!"

The door flew open and in swaggered Sergeant Terse, like a sheriff from the old Wild West, with deputies O'Keefe and Reidy scuttling along behind. Reidy had only recently returned to active service, having spent some months convalescing after a nasty incident involving a deranged female gangster. He'd only been persuaded to return to work by a gypsy fortune teller, who'd told him he had a 'lucky face' and sold him a sprig of 'lucky heather'.

"Where's the manager?" asked Terse in his usual no-nonsense manner.

"He's out," said Larry, "can I help?"

"Are you in charge?" asked Terse.

"Yes," said Larry.

"And you would be?" asked Terse.

"Larry Martin, cab controller,"

"You'll do," said Terse, handing him a warrant. "As I'm sure you know, Larry, this firm's breaking every rule in the book. We've got a court order to remove all your radio equipment and to arrest all your staff. Any questions?"

Larry gaped. Mehmet, who'd been smoking his hookah pipe in the back room and who'd overheard everything, emerged in a blue funk holding a baseball bat.

"Get out of my office, you heathens!" cried Mehmet. "Or I'll kick you out! Ram-A-Jam Taxis provide a good service, ask anyone. Everyone loves Ram-A-Jam."

"Look, mate," said Terse, "I'm only doing my duty. You hand over the transmitter and come quietly and everything will be fine."

Mehmet took a swipe at him with the baseball bat. Terse ducked and the bat connected with Reidy, who was looking the other way at the time.

"Aaaaarghhh! Me head!" cried Reidy, doubling up in pain.

"So sorry," said Mehmet, "I was trying to hit the other policeman."

"You shouldn't have done that, sunshine," snapped Terse,

removing the baton from his belt and swinging it at Mehmet's head. Mehmet jumped out of the way just in time and the baton came crashing down on the end of the controller's console, smashing part of the equipment.

"What have you done to my expensive equipment, you mad fool!" wailed Mehmet. Larry meanwhile had jumped onto the floor and started crawling away into the back room, heading for the exit.

"Grab the equipment, lads!" cried Terse.

"Oh no you don't!" cried Mehmet, taking another swipe at Terse with his bat.

Terse sidestepped the attack with his usual aplomb and as Mehmet sailed past him he swung a well judged kick after him, deflecting the bulky Turk into the crouching figure of Reidy, who was just getting up from the floor.

"Ooooofffff!" exclaimed Reidy as he collided headlong with the wall.

Mehmet collapsed into a heap, groaning, and Constable O'Keefe quickly slipped the handcuffs on him and read him his rights.

"Get the rest of the equipment together, Reidy, there's a good lad," said Terse. "I'll collect that joker, Larry Martin from the back room," he added. While Reidy was trying to recover sufficiently from his injuries to carry out the sergeant's orders and Terse was in action down the corridor, the radio transmitter crackled briefly into life again.

"No show, Larry" said a familiar voice. "I'm sitting outside the *King's Head* in Crouch End, but there's no sign of an Al Caholic."

Part Twenty-Six

Love is a many splendoured thing

Mike arrived back at 792A Finchley Road to find the front door off its hinges but held loosely in place by, what looked like, a complete roll of red and yellow crime scene marker tape. There were boot marks all over the door's paintwork so he assumed that the police had paid them a call. Climbing the stairs to the office he wondered briefly what had happened to Boltini and when he could expect a return visit from Terse.

Mike sat in Hymie's chair and put his feet up on the desk. Ah, the joys of being your own boss. The bloody chaos of the last few weeks was finally beginning to coagulate into some kind of deranged sense. As so often before, the simplest explanation, however absurd, was nearly always right; what had seemed at first to be just another missing magician investigation, had turned out to be a battle royal between two groups of wand-wavers who hated each others guts. His only concern was that the final punch-up had yet to take place and, as brave as he was, it wasn't really *his* fight. He was a great believer in minding his own business and Stonehenge had never been on his list of places to visit before you die, especially if it turned out to be last on the list.

The door downstairs collapsed loudly against the wall as Hymie breezed in with a huge devil-may-care smile on his face.

"This is it, Mike, I'm in love!" exclaimed the mushy detective.

"Hymie, we need to talk," said Mike.

"But first, I've gotta tell you about the girl of my dreams," continued Hymie. "She's simply stunning in every way."

"That's great, mate, but I have urgent news. The magicians have been round."

"Magicians? Who cares about magicians when you have a cool car and a beautiful girlfriend?" enthused Hymie. "By the way, what happened to the front door? We're not made of money you know."

"It turns out that those *lawyers* who got us out of the police station were really *The Amazing Harvey* and his assistant, Boltini," said Mike.

"Really?" said Hymie, throwing himself down on the settee.

"Yes, although it turns out that Boltini bats for the other side," continued Mike.

"You mean he's gay?" asked Hymie.

"No, you nurk, he works for the Red Square," explained Mike.

"Have you been sniffing the Domestos again?" asked Hymie, suspiciously.

"Look, H, there's no time to lose. It grieves me to say it but we've got to go to Stonehenge and it's gotta be now."

"Since when were you interested in ancient history, me old china?" asked Hymie. "You're making about as much sense as Terse on a bad day," he added.

"OK, Hymie, listen. There are two organisations, one called the Magic Triangle, the *good guys*, and one called the Red Square, the *bad guys*, right? They're both chock full of magicians and they hate each others guts. Now, the guy we were trying to find…"

"Harvey?" asked Hymie.

"That's right, Harvey; well, he's one of the good guys. Redrum and Boltini on the other hand…" continued Mike.

"Boltini?" wondered Hymie.

"The skinny guy with glasses who pretended to be Harvey's assistant," explained Mike.

"Oh, him," said Hymie.

"Yeah, well, he's working for the bad guys. Anyway, it seems as if the Square…" began Mike.

"Bad guys?" interrupted Hymie.

"Yep, as I was saying, the *Square*, which was behind the recent magician murders by the way, has kidnapped a load of magicians and is planning to polish them all off tonight at Stonehenge. Now, I know what you're thinking," said Mike.

"You mean, when are we gonna run into the *Green Rectangle?*" asked Hymie.

Mike fixed his senior partner with a look so belligerent that Goldman quickly fell silent. "Some of us have been working our butts off while you've been chasing birds," he snapped.

"Hold on there, Murphy!" exclaimed Hymie. "For a start, she's not a *bird* but a wonderful, divine, angel in human form, and for the record, I've been working too. I ran into some nut job last night in a coffee bar who also started blathering on about the Red Square. He gave me a blank cheque and asked me to help him find a bomb. I didn't take it seriously at the time, why would I? Besides, why would *anyone* want to go looking for a bomb? But now it all seems to fit into the shambles that is this case," concluded Hymie.

Mike rubbed his chin. "It just keeps getting more and more mysterious," he said. "But one thing's for sure…"

"I agree," said Hymie. "This isn't a job for us any longer, it's a job for Inspector Ray Decca of Goon Squad."

Mike nodded. He'd narrowly avoided admitting that Boltini had held him at gunpoint in their own offices because he could imagine the effect on Goldman and he wasn't about to blow it now.

"Only a damn fool policeman chasing promotion would be stupid enough to follow a group of madmen with a bomb to Stonehenge," said Hymie. "But how are we gonna get Decca to believe what's going on?" he added.

"That's what I was wondering," said Mike, "but then Harvey mentioned that we were being tailed by about half the police in North London."

"Are you sure?" asked Hymie.

"Just take a look out of the window, mate," said Mike. Hymie obliged. "Can you see a green florist's van?" asked Mike.

"Check," said Hymie.

"Well, at 12.15pm a guy from Domino's Pizza delivered three of their finest to the occupants of that van so, unless cut flowers need Margheritas, I'm guessing there are three cops in there," said Mike.

"Hah!" said Hymie. "Well I never."

"And that's not all," said Mike. "Do you see an ice-cream van?"

"Mr Sloppy?" asked Hymie.

"That's right, soppy," said Mike. "Well, apart from the obvious question of who buys ice-cream when it's minus three degrees out there, some kid actually did try to buy one earlier and a big guy with a crew cut opened the serving hatch and told him to piss off," added Mike.

"Great," said Hymie. "So we just have to open the window and shout down to them that we're going to Stonehenge, and we're in business."

"No, I'm afraid we'll have to go," said Mike. "It's the only way to be sure they get there. If we're lucky we'll be able to take a detour out of there when we get near."

Hymie looked doubtful. "You know I'm not much of a traveller," he said.

"Look, Goldman, we're talking Wiltshire not Outer Mongolia. Besides, I thought you loved driving that new heap of junk of yours," said Mike.

A blissful look flitted briefly across Hymie's face. "That's true," he said, "the Fleetwood could do with a spin." Then his face clouded over again as he remembered something.

"But don't you remember Madame Za Za's prediction, Mike?"

Mike had forgotten every word of it five minutes after leaving her flat. "Nope," he said. "It was all a load of baloney...something about a giant midget throwing stones at two policemen," he said.

"Nonesense, mate, she was right on the money; two policemen standing over a body while a magician casts spells over some giant rocks," recalled Hymie.

"Exactly," said Mike, irritably. "It was the kind of vague meaningless bullshit that could mean practically anything."

"Mike, get real, buddy. Giant rocks? Where else could it be but Stonehenge?" asked Hymie. Mike fell silent. He knew when he was beaten and didn't see the point in arguing any longer now that it was time for decisive action.

"OK, Goldman, I get it, but that just means we need to go and quickly. That's the only way we'll get the Fuzz there in time," said Mike, standing up and putting on his coat. "Have you got satnav in the all-American rust bucket?"

Hymie frowned and lowered his head. It wasn't so much that he was fed up of having his dream car abused as the realisation that he simply didn't want to go. He didn't want to walk into a trap or put his life at risk for nothing now that he had something, or someone, to lose. He looked cagily at Mike, now heading for the stairs, and finally realised that he didn't have any choice.

"It's OK, Mike, there's a road map in the glove compartment," he said.

Minutes later the two unlikely heroes climbed into the 1969 Fleetwood, revved up its monstrous engine and disappeared down the Finchley Road in a cloud of purple smoke.

Part Twenty-Seven

The need to know

Inspector Decca lay asleep across the desk in his office in Met Towers. His eyelids twitched uncontrollably as he dreamt about the rise and rise of data. Everything came down to data; more and more people, creating more and more reports on more and more other people, engaged in more and more pointless activities. Take the internet: when he was a kid, all the lads played football down the park. Now they sat at home in front of a screen playing computer games. What was that all about? Even Hymie Goldman had more sense than to waste his time playing computer games and he was virtually retarded. Then there were all the social media; more and more people making contacts or 'friends' who they would probably never meet and would probably loathe if they did. Besides, it was all a kind of cyber illusion; none of it was *real*. Sad really but eventually human kind would evolve into a race of blobs with two fingers to operate a computer console.

"Chief, Chief, wake up!" cried Terse, shaking the inspector awake.

"We'er, what?" snapped Decca. "What is it, Terse?"

Terse looked terrible. Leaning against the wall to stay upright, with bloodshot eyes and bedraggled hair, he looked like a man who'd been living on takeaways and hadn't slept for three days, which strangely enough he hadn't.

"Good news, sir. We've found Goldman and Murphy. They seem to be heading for Stonehenge," said Terse.

"They haven't become hippies have they?" asked Decca, who hadn't slept for a week.

"Not as far as I know, sir," said Terse.

"No, they probably haven't got enough hair between them to make one hippy," said Decca. "They weren't dressed as druids, I suppose?" he asked.

"Druids, sir?" said Terse, "I wouldn't know, sir. They just looked like the couple of scruffy gits of old," he added, gazing with concern at the Chief, who seemed to be losing the plot.

"Where are they now, Terse?" asked Decca.

"Heading down the M3 towards Salisbury, sir. We've got a helicopter and a couple of unmarked cars following them," added Terse.

"So what makes you think they're heading for Stonehenge of all places? It doesn't sound like one of their regular haunts to me," said Decca.

"They left a note on the door of their office at 792A Finchley Road, Chief," said Terse.

"I suppose it said 'Gone to Stonehenge, Back Soon' eh Terse?" said Decca, sarcastically.

"Yes, sir," said Terse, "how did you know?"

Decca looked at him doubtfully. "So, they're expecting us to follow them, I suppose," he said.

"I expect so, sir," agreed Terse.

"But, why?" snapped Decca. "What the hell are those two idiots up to now? It all seems a bit fishy to me, Terse, but I dare say we'll find out soon enough. Get onto the Wiltshire Constabulary and tip them off that we're expecting an Alpha One emergency at Stonehenge later today. You never know, they may already have it under observation, but even if they don't, where Goldman leads can trouble be far behind?" asked Decca.

"No, sir," agreed Terse.

"Then get me an unmarked car, Terse, something fast and ask the special weapons officer to join us. We'll need to be suitably tooled up;

if Goldman's going to Stonehenge we could be on the verge of World War Three," said Decca. "Either that or a punch-up with some hippies," he added.

"Yes, sir," said Terse, who liked nothing better.

The phone on Decca's desk began to ring. He rolled his eyes skywards as he picked up the handset. It was sure to be some smart-alec boyfriend of his ex-wife's trying to wind him up or the Chief Inspector bugging him with questions he didn't have the answers to. Nothing made sense any more: his ex-wife, his job, the football results. Nothing. He opened his mouth to speak then thought better of it and slammed the handset back down.

"Let's go and kick some ass, Barry," said Decca, "and if it's Hymie Goldman's then so much the better."

"Yes, sir!" replied Terse enthusiastically, unaccustomed to such wild displays of bonhomie from the Chief.

Part Twenty-Eight

Flotsam and Jetsam

If you want to drive from North London to Salisbury in a hurry there's no finer road than the M3. Frankly, you'd be mad to go any other way, even if you could find another route. Other roads may be more scenic, less noisy and less damaging to the environment but nothing so far invented can surpass it for directness and speed of travel. If you're fortunate enough to have already passed Farnborough and thus to have broken the back of your journey, and are in dire need of a shot of caffeine before the ordeal that is Basingstoke, then you couldn't do better than to visit Fleet Services.

It's true that the ambiance leaves something to be desired; with its grim, functional, shed-like architecture, like a headlong collision between Bauhaus, Hammer horror and a nissen hut. With the fragrant aroma of diesel wafting tantalisingly over the half-empty lorry park and the hordes of screaming kids dragging their disspirited parents off to McDonalds for a happy meal, nowhere could be more alluring to the seasoned metropolitan traveller of today's Britain.

What price to enjoy the cold fries and warm sandwiches? The chance to re-fill your tank with super-taxed petrol or your bladder with anaemic coffee? What price the chance to take a leak in the convivial surroundings of the world class toilets or the range and quality of the well-stocked shops? These things, of course, are beyond price, and perhaps it's as well not to ask the price as a shock is surely bad for the digestion.

At Fleet Services you can buy a newspaper, a book of twenty year old crossword puzzles, some overboiled sweets or a packet of tin tacks (not to be confused with the mints with a similar name for obvious reasons). You can sit in the cafeteria and watch the world go by; fat and poor, rich and thin, hirsute or follically challenged, famous or unknown, the flotsam and jetsam of humanity; all desperate to get off the motorway for a break and shortly afterwards all too desperate to re-join it.

Fleet Services never closes, Fleet Services welcomes all. Fleet Services is more than a place, it's a state of mind; rather like the prison of the same name or the *Hotel California*, 'you can check out any time you like, but you can never leave'.

Hymie and Mike sat staring at the froth on top of their coffees in Fleet Services, wondering what on earth they were doing there at the world's end and when the government had introduced the new super-tax on coffee.

Outside on the tarmac, three unmarked police cars pulled into the service station car park. In the black Vauxhall Insignia V6, Sergeant Terse turned off his ignition and flicked a switch on his police radio.

"Bravo One this is Charlie Three, can you read me, over?" he said.

"Come in Charlie Three, this is Bravo One," came the reply. "Stop pratting around, Terse, I'm parked right next to you, man," said Inspector Decca. "Get off the police radio frequency and see if you can find Goldman and Murphy. They're inside that square building over there," said Decca, pointing, "probably having a cup of coffee. How hard can it be, Terse? It's *Goldman and Murphy* not Al-Qaeda and this is a ruddy motorway service station not central London!"

"Right you are, sir," said Terse into his handset. "Over and out, Bravo One" he said, switching his radio off. He climbed out of the car to speak to his junior colleague DC Collins, who was already returning from a foray into the main service station concourse.

"Two men answering the description of the suspects just crossed the footbridge to the eastbound carriageway, sarge," said Collins.

"What, a tall well-set guy and a short scruffy bloke in a tatty leather jacket?" asked Terse, taken aback.

"Yes, sarge," confirmed Constable Collins.

Terse scratched his head. This made no sense at all. "You mean they've got wind of the fact we're here?" he asked.

"Could be, sarge. They looked like they were planning to climb into the back of a lorry heading back to London. Shall we apprehend them?"

"You can tell all that can you, Collins? You can tell what they're thinking just by their shifty behaviour?" asked Terse.

"Well, I've got a psychology degree, see, sarge," said Collins.

"And you know where you can stick it, mate," said Terse. "I dunno where they get 'em from, I really don't," he muttered to himself as he signalled to his remaining colleagues to join him.

"Right you lot, Collins has spotted Goldman and Murphy heading over the footbridge. Quickly, everyone over there to collar them before they hitch a ride back to the Smoke," barked Terse.

Decca wound down the window of his car. "Carry on, sergeant, I'll just grab a cuppa and be with you in a minute or two," he said.

"It's OK, Chief, I'll get them," said Terse, sending the five other officers off in pursuit, so he could have a breather. They ran into the concourse, raced up the stairs to the footbridge and disappeared out of sight while Terse walked over to the kiosk to collect two teas.

Hymie and Mike sat watching incredulously as the coppers ran past them without any hint of recognition. Fortunately, Terse had missed them too as he'd blundered into a group of Japanese tourists on the way back to their coach and narrowly avoided spilling all of his drinks as he passed them.

"I think we'd better go," said Hymie, as the last policeman went by.

"I haven't quite finished my coffee," said Mike, raising the cup to his mouth.

Suddenly Inspector Decca appeared at the main entrance doors looking for Terse and his drink. Mike squatted down behind a plastic pot-plant and pulled Goldman along with him.

"I've finished now," he said, placing his cup inside the plant pot. Decca was crossing the concourse floor to inspect the detective novels in the news kiosk when Terse appeared with his half-empty cup of tea. While they exchanged pleasantries, Mike and Hymie quickly slipped past them, holding open newspapers in front of their faces. They reached the doors undetected, crossed the car park and climbed into the Fleetwood. Decca and Terse returned to the car park shortly afterwards. They were standing on the tarmac watching the road bridge when Terse's police radio crackled into action with the latest news from Collins.

"They've apprehended the suspects, sir," said Terse.

Goldman and Murphy drove slowly past, heading for the feeder lane to the M3 west, and waved comically at Decca.

"I can see that, Terse," said the Inspector, irritably. He stood seething at the kerb but could do nothing to stop them.

"Well, at least we know they'll be following us," said Mike.

"Yeah, but it was dangerously close," said Hymie. "If they'd arrested us there we'd have never made it to Stonehenge, and those magicians are depending on us."

Part Twenty-Nine

In Stonehenge no one can hear you scream

It was late in the afternoon and the sun was beginning to set as the Fleetwood coasted down the A303 to Stonehenge. Hymie and Mike sat in silence, lulled by the sound-dampening snow outside and the faint hiss of slush running off their tyres.

"I wonder where the Fuzz have got to?" wondered Mike. "We haven't seen 'em since leaving Fleet Services."

"Oh, they'll turn up. It's not as if they don't know where we're heading," said Hymie. "Besides, how hard can it be to tail a multi-coloured American car the size of a small town?"

"You're not wrong, H," said Mike. "I did see a chopper in the distance as we left the M3 but it's been eerily quiet ever since. Anyway, as you say, if they wanted to find us they'd have no problems."

"It's about time we turned off this road and headed back to civilisation," said Hymie. "I mean, we don't want to find ourselves at Stonehenge by accident, do we? Have a look at the map, Mike."

Mike shrugged. "I kinda thought we'd have to go through with it," he said.

"But you *agreed* we'd hightail it out of there," said Hymie, anxiously. "We were only trying to lead the police to Stonehenge."

"Yeah, but how else are we gonna be sure the Red Square don't do something stupid?" asked Mike.

"Why is that *our* problem?" asked Hymie. "The world's full of loony organisations doing daft things, most of them governments, but what chance have we got of stopping them?"

"We have to try," said Mike. "We'll just go and have a look, wait until the police arrive and then push off, right?" he suggested.

Hymie tightened his grip on the steering wheel and sighed like a deflating tyre. It didn't look like he had much choice. It was always the same; as one door closed, another slammed in your face! He nodded reluctantly.

When they reached the turn off for Stonehenge via the A344 they were startled to find that the road had been closed. A makeshift barrier had been erected in the middle of the carriageway and a red warning sign said 'Chemical Spill, Keep Out!' to which some joker had appended the words 'No Hippies. This means you!' in green spray paint.

"Whadda ya reckon?" wondered Mike.

"I've been ignoring 'Keep Out' signs most of my life, so it's a bit late to start now," said Hymie, putting his foot down on the accelerator. The old Fleetwood groaned, then roared, then lurched forward with its wheels spinning, demolishing the sign and the barrier as it ploughed on through the slush.

"Goldman, your driving sucks!" said Mike.

"Kicks ass, don't you mean, Mike?" corrected Hymie.

Mike smirked. "They're not that far apart really," he said. He retrieved his old break-top Webley revolver from his inside pocket, flicked it open and loaded each of the six chambers with a bullet from his right hand jacket pocket.

"Look, Mike, I don't want no one getting shot, right?" said Hymie.

"Fine, I'll just have to shoot everyone we meet then," agreed Mike, "that ought to do it," he added, putting the loaded weapon back in his jacket pocket.

They arrived at the car park and climbed out of the car. The place was deserted and eerily, almost deathly, quiet. As they walked along the pathway in the fading light the monument hove into view; four groups of snow-covered stones like giant snowmen, enclosed in a circular ditch. The large blue sarcen stones seemed to stand guard in the chill winter evening against some unknown terror, as they had for countless millennia and would, in all likelihood, do for many more.

"So, is this it?" said Mike. "Just a bunch of giant rocks in the middle of Salisbury Plain? I was expecting something more," he added.

"More?" scoffed Hymie. "What did you expect? A bevy of naked virgins pole-dancing around the stones while a bunch of drunken druids looked on, chanting ancient football songs? Or a chorus of dancing girls perhaps, high-kicking their way across Salisbury Plain? Or maybe even a herd of marauding wildebeest? This place is a world heritage site, Mike, you have to take it as you find it."

"Well, you can't really miss it, I suppose," conceded Mike, grudgingly. He patted the Webley in his pocket for reassurance. "Come on, H, let's get this show on the road."

Hymie looked stricken. "What, without Decca and Terse?" he asked.

"Well, they haven't done us a whole lot of good so far," said Mike.

"I know, but at least they have plenty of back up," said Hymie.

"They've always got my back up anyway," he smirked. "All we have is you and a gun. I'm a spent force once I've made a few wisecracks and run off to hide," he added.

"Don't sell yourself short, H, your wisecracks would stop an army of psychopaths with uzis dead in their tracks at fifty paces," said Mike.

Hymie looked at him in surprise.

"Only kidding," said Mike, "but at least you're very good at hiding," he concurred. "Besides, we're JP Confidential, we're *the best*, it says so in our marketing literature."

"You don't mean to tell me you've fallen for that old pony?" said Hymie.

"No, of course not," said Mike. "But I'm cold, wet, and in the middle of nowhere and I just want to get World War Three over with so I can go home and enjoy what's left of Christmas!" he cried, walking off towards the centre of the stone circles.

"Mike, come back. You can't leave me here on my own. What

about the Red Square? What about the chemical spill?" asked Hymie. "It could be toxic. You know I break out in a terrible rash at the slightest trace of chemicals," he added, desperately.

Mike paused briefly, looked blankly at his pitiful colleague then headed off again. Hymie shrugged then ran after his outsized business partner, eventually catching up with him as Mike suddenly fell to the ground.

"Ah, the old army training eh?" said Hymie, squatting down beside him.

"No, I'm tying my shoe lace, mate, how about you?" said Mike.

"I thought I heard something," bluffed Hymie, in a whisper.

They gazed out across the historic vista of the standing stones. Backlit by a large orange sun, gradually setting in the west, they appeared less like a part of the real world and more like some outlandish dreamscape. A thin plume of smoke began to rise from a fire in the distance.

"I don't like the look of that," said Mike.

"Me neither, we really should call for back-up," said Hymie.

"Here," said Mike, handing Hymie a rubber cosh and a heavy brass knuckleduster. "You're it, H, stay close on my tail," he said, walking slowly forwards. Through the lengthening shadows of dusk, the two detectives slowly crossed the field that lead to the stones, attempting all the while to keep a low profile. Soon a semi-circle of tents appeared from out of the gloom. One tent stood out from the others by the opulence of its scarlet satin trim, its grandiose scale and by the two armed guards posted outside with sub-machine guns.

The tents were pitched on the far side of the stones with a large bonfire immediately in front of them, emitting the same thin trail of smoke they'd recently observed. The fire itself could only just have been lit as the flames hadn't spread to the main section yet. The core of the fire seemed to comprise of a stack of old wooden furniture, dotted about with bizarre hooded figures, like dinner-suited scarecrows.

"We don't have any grenades, I suppose?" asked Mike, wistfully.

"No, I gave the last one to my Auntie Ada for Christmas," said Hymie.

"Shame," said Mike. "How is she?"

"Still recovering in hospital," said Hymie.

As they inched forward to the very edge of the outer stone circle, they realised that they were already in too deep and had passed the point of no return. There's never a cop around when you want one, thought Hymie, who'd never wanted one before.

An army of red-coated minions milled around the stones, like a swarm of red ants in the centre of the circle. On their left flank, a kangaroo court seemed to be in progress, passing sentence on the Square's enemies without recourse to evidence, facts or presumably, justice. On the right, a bedraggled line of convicted magicians in dinner suits were being lead in chains to the altar stone to meet their doom. Dumbstruck, Hymie and Mike watched in horror as the grand inquisitor, robed entirely in red and wearing a devil mask, asked the bowed-headed victim at the front of the line if he wanted to say anything before his sentence was carried out.

"I'm no criminal, I'm Domino Dave," said the cringing character in the dirty dinner jacket. "I'm a children's entertainer for Christsakes, let me out of here!"

Dave started fishing desperately in his pocket for something to support his claims but could only produce two dominoes.

"Sadly deluded right till the end," sneered the grand inquisitor.

Suddenly incensed, Dave pulled a concealed wand from his back pocket and rammed it up his tormentor's left nostril. "Take that, you red bastard!" he cried, before he was clubbed to the ground by baseball bat-wielding henchmen.

"Aaaaargh!" shrieked the grand inquisitor in agony. "I saw his act once, it was an abomination!" he cried, callously, once he'd collected himself together. Dave collapsed unconscious to the floor. Two attendants picked up his crumpled body, covered his head with an old sack hood and dragged him off.

A tall well-dressed man with white hair followed him in the

queue. As he approached the grand inquisitor, Mike recognised him as *The Amazing Harvey*.

"Afraid to show your face, eh?" said Harvey, contemptuously. "I'm not surprised, but don't expect to have it all your own way, slimeball. We have reinforcements coming any minute and it's the Square that will burn in hell before the day is out, not the Triangle!" he cried. He pulled a deck of Bicycle playing cards from out of his jacket pocket and spread them in a fan. "Pick a card, any card," he said, proffering them to the grand inquisitor from force of habit.

The inquisitor removed his mask with a flourish and cursed him.

"Damn you, Harvey! I've waited a long time for this day and there's a special place reserved for you on top of the bonfire," he snarled, removing his spectacles to wipe away the condensation. It was Boltini.

"I always had my doubts about you, James Bolton," said Harvey, calmly. "I think it was the fact that you never once blinked in all the time we worked together."

"You're blinking mad, mate," said Boltini, with a sneer. He nodded twice and a gang of red-coated henchmen descended on Harvey, crushing him to the ground. He was dragged away with a sack over his head, pulling the flags of all nations from his coat-sleeves, as he disappeared to join his colleagues.

"My God, they're building a funeral pyre!" cried Hymie, slowly catching on.

Mike was ahead of him. "Not for much longer," he said, standing up. "I've got a plan, H."

"What happened to plans A to G?" asked Hymie.

Mike grimaced. "It's hardly the time for bad jokes, Goldman."

"There's nothing wrong with our usual plan," said Hymie. "You shoot the lot of them while I run off and hide," he added, trying to lighten the atmosphere.

Mike smiled. "Not this time, mate, we're massively outnumbered. Look, I'll try and work my way around to the leader's tent and see if I can get a hostage while you go and get the police. No pressure, H, but if you don't make it back in time I should jack in the detective racket if I were you and go back to being an electrician."

Hymie shook his head. "You've never seen my re-wiring," he said, dismissively. "It's more lethal than your left hook. Don't worry though, you can count on me, Mike," he added, with conviction. Then he turned and ran, as fast as he could, back to the car. Once inside the Fleetwood he called Decca on his mobile phone and told him in as few words as possible what was happening. Decca confirmed that they were already on their way to Stonehenge and told him not to do anything stupid, which made Terse laugh uproariously in the background, or so it sounded to Hymie.

The smoke plume was beginning to rise more prominently into the chill night sky. Hymie clenched his fists until his knuckles stood out white in the car's dark interior. Damn it! He couldn't sit idly by while those poor magicians fried, or while the best business partner he'd ever had, come to think of it, the *only* business partner he'd ever had, Mike was in mortal danger. He may be as much use as a chocolate teapot at a diabetics' convention but he'd have to do *something*! If not, he may as well be the tea-boy as the proprietor of JP Confidential. He strode manfully out across the field once more with the steely glint of determination in his eyes. Red Square? Hah! he'd soon hammer them into a mangled oblong sort of shape. Too late, he realised he'd been under surveillance the whole time as a group of assailants descended on him from out of the shadows.

"You'll never take me alive, you red devils!" cried Hymie.

"That's the general idea, ducky!" snapped the dwarf at the front of the group, who seemed to be in charge.

"You're not Mal the Fag, by any chance?" asked Hymie. "Mike said you were a useless ponce."

Seething with rage the diminutive figure leapt onto him, grabbing him by the throat and throttling the wise-cracking detective until he could hardly breathe. Hymie lunged out with the rubber cosh and knuckle-duster Mike had given him, narrowly escaping strangulation, but before he could escape the rest of the gang set about him.

Something hard struck the back of Hymie's head and a searing pain shot through him. He staggered forward a few feet and wondered if this was the end. He was drifting in and out of consciousness now, reeling unsteadily on his feet. He could have sworn he heard the whoop whoop sound of a chopper blade overhead and then a blinding spotlight fell on him from above. If it was the police then great but they'd come far, far too late for him. For him it was all over. He fell with a thud onto the cold hard ground and lay perfectly still.

Mike battled on, all unknowing. Overcoming the setbacks of being large and unwieldy, he'd skirted around the edge of the stone circles with panther-like grace until he'd arrived at the head honcho's tent. As luck would have it, one of the guards appeared to be taking a leak behind a standing stone a short distance away, so Mike seized his chance and quickly pistol-whipped the solitary guard with a well-aimed blow from the butt of his trusty Webley. He waited in the shadows for the return of the second guard before repeating the process and leaving the two of them trussed up like a pair of Christmas turkeys in the back of a trailer parked conveniently nearby. As every second passed, the flames on the bonfire snaked ever higher and the prospects of rescuing the magicians seemed to ebb further and further away.

Mike pulled back the hammer on his Webley Double Action, pushed through the tent flaps with it held tightly in his shooting hand and prepared to deliver his ultimatum to the Square's commander.

Inside the tent, a vivacious young woman with dark curly hair sat behind a fold-up table in her red jump-suit, watching him coolly.

"You!" he said.

She smiled bemusedly at him. "Who were you expecting, the Wicked Witch of the West?" she replied.

"If the name fits," said Mike.

All further conversation, however, was lost in the cacophony from outside the tent as the police made their grand, if belated, entrance with three helicopters, an armoured car and a fleet of patrol vehicles at exactly the same time as Hymie was making his last stand. Sirens blared, chopper blades whooped and gallons of water were jettisoned onto the bonfire from above as the perpetrators ran in all directions like headless chickens. Decca was determined to rain on the Red Square's parade. Promotion beckoned.

Mike turned back towards the entrance to the tent and poked his head out through the flaps to see what was happening. "The police!" he cried. "That was quick work, Hymie!" He turned back to gloat over the Red Square's imminent defeat but all he saw was a cloud of red dust. The woman in red was gone.

Outside on the field of battle, Decca and Terse had been pinned down by gunfire. Three of their patrol cars had exploded into flames and several police officers lay injured on the ground.

"Terse, take half of the men and get behind the tents," cried Decca. "We need to trap them in a pincer movement or we'll lose them in the dark."

Terse headed off with a dozen officers in riot gear. He was in his element at last, now that the gloves were off and the adrenalin pumping, he quickly deployed his troops to best effect, forming an outer perimeter fence around the tents.

"Don't forget, men," cried Terse, "wait till you can see the whites of their eyes, then beat the crap out of them!"

The choppers flew in, dispersing tear gas canisters in the centre of Red Square operations. The gang members scattered and ran, either into the waiting batons and fists of Terse and his team or towards Inspector Decca, still crouching by the burning police cars.

A few of the gang members were still firing at the police and Decca became increasingly concerned, not only for the safety of his men, but about the damage to the ancient stones. He lifted his loud hailer and stood up behind his car.

"Oi, you lot!" he cried. "Don't you realise this is a *world heritage site!* Put down your weapons and give yourselves up or it'll be the worse for you!" he shouted with conviction.

As the choppers flew past over the battlefield again, shining their spotlights down on the assembled gang members as they did so, it was clear that the miscreants were thinking about it. Decca continued to exploit his theme. "Do you *really* want your families to know you wrecked Stonehenge? It's only been here for a few thousand years, you know. I expect when you get to court even the judges would take a dim view of that!"

It was a defining moment and Decca knew it. After some grumbling and dissent in the ranks, the Red Square finally laid down their weapons and surrendered. Although there had been casualties on both sides, Decca and Terse could take satisfaction in a job well done and look forward to the promotion they so richly deserved.

Mike, meanwhile, who'd been scouring the pre-historic building site for some time, looking for Hymie, finally came upon his prostrate figure as he headed back to see if he'd simply high-tailed it out of there in the Fleetwood. He knelt down anxiously beside Hymie's body and tried to take his pulse. For a moment time seemed to stand still in that desolate place.

"He's dead!" cried Mike, pounding on the snow covered ground with his massive fists. He stood up, consumed with rage, and glowered at the retreating ranks of the Red Square. "You've killed him, you bastards!" he shouted, tears welling in his eyes. "He may have been the worst business partner in the world and his personal hygiene may have left a lot to be desired but he was only here because I asked him!" snarled Mike.

A police medic walked over to Goldman's body, stooped down and checked again for signs of life. "Actually, he's alive!" he cried. "Get him a stretcher, someone."

Mike fell silent. "Oh, well, my mistake, no one's perfect," he said at last, blowing his nose to wipe away his tears. "Thank God the dopey sod's still with us, 'cause if there's one job I definitely wouldn't want, it's his," he added, following the stretcher to the waiting helicopter.

Part Thirty

Quark, Quark, Quark!

At New Scotland Yard the evidence had finally begun to catch up with the Red Square. Weapons, prints, bodies, dental records, every one told a tale. No longer just a bunch of faceless ghosts, the Red Square had become a list of suspects on the run. Most importantly, they were all men and women with bank accounts who'd been paid by electronic bank transfer, and in this computer-controlled world every payment left a tiny digital trail behind. While the identity of its leaders remained a mystery the net was rapidly closing in on the Square's financiers, the Millennium Group.

As for Hymie and Mike, the powers that be had decided that the last thing they needed was a media circus and that the best way to avoid one was to keep those two clowns out of the courts. They were told to keep out of trouble or else and quietly shown the door. At least, *Mike* was shown the door; the door to the Fleetwood, and told to piss off. Goldman, who'd been reduced to a semi-vegetative state and was having a job identifying how many fingers Terse was holding up, continued to stare at the ceiling of the Royal Free Hospital, too dazed to object. After a couple of days of hospital food and daytime TV therapy, however, his self-preservation instinct kicked in and he phoned Mike, pleading to be picked up in the Fleetwood.

With Mike at the wheel and Hymie fiddling with his bandaged head in the back of the car, the conversation finally wound its way back to Stonehenge.

"So, what happened to you, H?" asked Mike.

"Someone hit me," said Hymie, helpfully.

"I can't blame them for that, I've often felt like doing it myself," said Mike, "but what were you doing at the time?" he asked.

"I'd just spoken to Decca on my mobile and I was coming back to find you," said Hymie.

"You were?" asked Mike, surprised.

"I was, and then wallop, all I saw was stars," added Hymie.

"So, I suppose you'll want to know what happened next?" asked Mike.

Hymie opened his mouth to speak then paused. "You know, Mike, I don't believe I do. You see, I'm tired, my head aches and I'm sure knowing how close we came to total disaster, as usual, won't make me feel any better."

Mike fell into a sulky silence. He'd lost count of the number of times he'd had to sit and listen to Goldman waffling on about some rubbish and now that *he* knew what had happened, while Goldman was completely clueless, it seemed a bit much that the dope didn't want to hear it.

"After you fell on your face," began Mike, "I battled my way into the leader's tent."

"It's OK, Mike, it's not necessary, really," said Hymie.

Mike fixed him with a stare that said 'shut up and listen or you're going straight back to A&E'.

"Fantastic," said Hymie.

"Exactly," said Mike. "Well, when I got in there, who d'ya think was there?" he asked.

"Father Christmas?" wondered Hymie.

"No, Ruby," said Mike.

Hymie's face fell. "You mean she was working for the Red Square?"

"I'm afraid so, H," said Mike. "In fact, she seemed to be in charge. Oh, and Harvey and Boltini were there too," he added. "Boltini turned out to be some kind of senior officer in the Square."

Hymie seemed to have lost all interest in the conversation. "Oh, I see," he said quietly.

They drove the rest of the way back to 792A Finchley Road in silence. Mike parked on the pavement outside and turned off the Fleetwood's eight cylinder engine.

"Did we have to come back here?" asked Hymie. "I thought, in the circumstances, you might let me crash at your flat over Christmas."

"Yeah, well, as long as you're paying for everything," said Mike, reluctantly. "I just need to check on Bacon first."

"What, that damned flea-bitten moggy?" asked Hymie.

"I know, I just can't bear to think of him being shut up in the office over Christmas," said Mike.

"Good point," agreed Hymie. "Imagine the smell if he was locked in for a few days, let alone a week."

"You're all heart," said Mike.

"I know," said Hymie. "I'm my own worst enemy."

They made their way up the threadbare stair carpet and into their empty office. There was no sign of a cat anywhere. What there was; slap bang in the middle of Hymie's desk, was a large cardboard box with a card label attached.

"Looks like Decca's sent you a Christmas prezzie, H," said Mike.

Hymie smiled. "We'd better check it's not ticking, Mike. I don't attract too many well-wishers, as you know."

"You can say that again," agreed Mike.

Hymie lifted up the attached card and read the inscription.

"This isn't much use to me any longer, Hymie, but it could make you a rich man, love Ruby X."

The far-away look played briefly over Goldman's gormless face before Mike called him back from his fool's paradise.

"Hellooo! Goldman! She was working for the *bad guys*, remember. It's probably a bomb or something similar," cried Mike in disbelief.

"There's nothing *similar* to a bomb, Mike," said Hymie. "Either it goes BOOM or it doesn't."

"Well, let's not put it to the test, mate," said Mike.

Hymie lifted the lid off the box to discover a large silver-coloured brick inside with one large red button in the middle. Engraved in italics next to the button were the words 'Do Not Press'.

"What do you think it is?" asked Mike. "A sandwich toaster?" Hymie picked up the metal brick and examined it more closely. "Errr… it's quite heavy," he said. "It might even be solid silver; we could sell it for scrap. I wonder what the button does?"

"I dunno, H, but if I were you I'd leave it well alone," said Mike. He reached out to take it away from his loopy partner but Hymie was already pressing the button.

"Noooooo!" cried Mike, jumping behind the settee with his fingers in his ears.

"Hello, I'm Daisy-Belle. Congratulations on activating me," said the device, as Mike hit the deck like an oversized sack of spuds.

"Hello, Daisy-Belle," said Hymie, a little surprised to find himself talking to a silver brick. "Are you a telephone answering machine?" he asked.

"Why, no, I'm a Series Alpha Quark Bomb," explained the device.

"No kidding," said Hymie with a hint of sarcasm. "Wouldn't you rather toast us two cheese sandwiches?" he asked, hopefully.

"No, my sole function is to create a black hole triggering complete gravitational collapse, whereupon all matter on earth will be sucked into a void for all eternity," said Daisy-Belle.

Mike had regained his composure sufficiently to stick his head up above the back of the settee and gawp at the device.

"Oh my God, it's *that* bomb!" said Hymie.

Mike looked at him with a pained expression in which curiosity, outrage and utter confusion battled without resolution. "You mean you knew there was a bomb on the loose and you *still* pressed the button?" asked Mike, aggrieved.

"Yeah, well, it was an easy mistake to make," said Hymie, defensively. "It didn't look like a bomb."

"You mean it didn't have the word 'BOMB' written on it in large capital letters?" asked Mike.

"Hang on a minute," said Hymie, "if this is a bomb, why hasn't it gone off?"

"Five minutes to detonation," said Daisy-Belle, helpfully.

"Ah," said Hymie, "how far away do you think we can get in five minutes, Mike?"

"However far it is, it won't be enough, you berk!" snapped Mike. "The only thing we can do is try to deactivate it. Try pressing the button again."

"What do you think this button is, Mike, a flamin' light-switch you can just turn on and off?" said Hymie, pressing the button again just in case. In the ensuing silence they dared to hope.

"You have already activated me, thank you," said Daisy-Belle.

Hymie began to perspire freely as a blind panic gripped him. His short-lived career as an electrician had been something he'd always tried to forget but now he was beginning to contemplate opening up Daisy-Belle to cut through her wires, assuming she had any. There had to be another way and fortunately there was; the moment passed.

"Listen to me, Daisy-Belle," said Hymie, "can you be de-activated?"

"Yes, my detonation sequence can be terminated if you tell me the eighteen digit code," said Daisy-Belle.

"Eighteen!" spluttered Hymie. It might just as well have asked him to climb to the top of Mount Everest while giving Murphy a piggy back.

"Four minutes to detonation," added Daisy-Belle, with complete indifference.

Hymie decided to try reasoning with the device. He removed his bandages to show how seriously he was taking matters. Mike meanwhile seemed to have lost the plot and was busily rummaging around in the cleaning cupboard.

"OK, Daisy-Belle, listen to me," said Hymie. "Why do you want to create a black hole?"

"It is my function."

"Yes, OK, but what purpose does your function serve?" asked Hymie.

"I am not programmed to answer your question, only to detonate," said Daisy-Belle.

Typical bloody woman! thought Hymie. "Look, I only activated you by mistake," he said, "so if you detonate you won't be providing a satisfactory service."

"Let me think about that," said the bomb. For what seemed an eternity nothing happened. Mike continued to rummage while Hymie sweated.

"This is hopeless," said Hymie, at last. "I'm going to call the bomb squad like I should've done in the first place."

"Step away from the telephone, fatso," said Daisy-Belle. "One minute to detonation."

"So what was all that crap about 'let me think about it'?" said Goldman, resentfully, seething from the unjustified personal abuse.

"Does not compute," said Daisy-Belle.

"Mike! It's all over! Curtains!" cried Hymie.

"I'm more of a blinds man, myself," said Mike, storming back into the room with a bucket full of warm soapy water, right on cue. He placed it on the floor by Hymie's desk before grabbing the Quark bomb and quickly dropping it into the water. It sank to the bottom, fizzing merrily as it went. Daisy-Belle's last words were "You bast.... Fzzzzzt!"

"How on earth did you know that would work?" asked Hymie, when it became clear that it had.

"Oh, intuition," said Mike. "I dropped my mobile phone down the bog last year and it never worked again so I assumed it would work with a Quark bomb too."

"You never cease to amaze me, Murphy," said Hymie.

"Oh, it was nothing," said Mike, modestly.

"So, about Christmas at your flat," began Hymie.

"It'll cost you, Goldman," said Mike, "but I do have a new dancing Santa decoration that I know you're gonna love," he added, leading the way outside to their waiting Fleetwood.

Part Thirty-One

A very personal Black Hole

In the penthouse suite of the tallest skyscraper in downtown Dallas, Tex Avery sat in the boardroom, drumming his fingers on the table with boredom, surrounded by his puppet Board. He was lamenting the failure of *Project Daisy-Belle,* as he had christened his scheme to destroy the world by sucking it into a black hole. A few days earlier they'd all been gathered at the appointed time at a hog roast on his ranch, waiting to meet their maker. However, other than the consumption of a tonne of scorched pork, nothing earth shattering had happened.

"D'ya think the bomb went off after all and we're just sitting here in heaven dreaming?" wondered Tex, removing his Stetson.

"Well, Papa Tex, wouldn't there be angels or something?" asked Sybil Cronk, Head of Marketing.

"You're right, my child, we've been let down again by those darn foreigners. I should've known they couldn't be relied on. Next time we'll use our own, home grown talent. Why, show me a man from anywhere in the world who can blow things up better than an American and I'll show you a damn liar!" snapped Tex.

He was gratified to see the rows of nodding heads around the table as he surveyed his fellow Board members.

"Hallelujah!" cried Forrest Hawks, Head of Resources, emphatically.

Tex's glance alighted on Dave Clarke, their British Head of

Accounting and Finance, and his face fell. There was something not quite right about the guy; he wasn't from Texas.

"How much money have we got left, Dave?" asked Tex.

Dave pressed a few keys at random on his calculator to lend weight to his prognosis. "It's not looking good, Tex," he said, quietly. How did you tell a Texan oil billionaire he was broke? wondered Dave. Preferably on a long distance call.

"Not good? But you're in charge of the finances, Dave, why not?" thundered Tex.

Dave toyed with the idea of telling the truth; that he just did as he was told like all the other muppets in Tex Towers, but realised it would be verging on insanity.

"Well, er, Tex," he replied, chewing his nails briefly, "I managed to stop some of the payments to the Red Square but someone in London's frozen our assets."

"God damn Limeys!" cried Tex, glaring at Dave.

"And we've started getting calls from some heavy duty agencies in the US," added Dave.

"Such as?" queried Tex.

"The CIA, the NSA, the FBI and the IRS," said Dave.

"But I have friends in all these organisations on the payroll," said Tex, dismissively.

"Yes, but we can't access any funds to pay them," blurted Dave.

"Dave, deal with it, buddy, or you'll be leaving us very soon!" said Tex.

"The CIA said they wanted to interview you *today*, Tex," continued Dave.

"Well, that's a terrible shame, Dave, 'cause I'm busy. Why don't they interview you, instead?" said Tex.

"Er, well, I don't know, er..." said Dave, who suddenly had a desperate desire to be somewhere else.

"It wasn't a question, Dave," said Tex. "Thank you laydees and gentlemen, I'm now calling this Board meeting to order," he added unequivocally. He stood up, put his Stetson back on his head and smiled at the assembled crowd of sycophants and hangers-on as he headed for a cupboard at the back of the room. Removing a key from the fob attached to his belt he unlocked the cupboard and removed a gunbelt containing two bright shiny Colt revolvers. He strapped on the belt and turned to face the Board.

"Blessed are the peacemakers, for they shall be called the sons of God!" cried Tex. "And what I got me here are a couple of Mr Colt's finest peacemakers!" he added.

"Why, Papa, what you gonna do?" asked Sybil Cronk, anxiously. Like others on the Board she'd reluctantly signed up for being sucked into a black hole for all eternity, but drew the line at dying in a hail of bullets.

"Why, child, this is Texas, and in Texas it's your God given right to defend your home from intruders," said Tex, checking that every chamber in each of his revolvers was loaded and ready to roll. "If the CIA think they can just waltz in here without an invitation they have another thing coming!" he added.

"Three black sedans just pulled into the car park," said Dave, who'd asked the security guard on the desk downstairs to text him as soon as any strange visitors arrived.

"Shred everything, Dave!" cried Tex. "Anything those goddamned heathens from the CIA could misconstrue as non-charitable activities anyhow! The rest of you good 'ol Texan boys, go getcha guns out of your desks, cars and offices and meet me in the lobby in ten. Let's give the CIA a warm Texan welcome."

The rest of the Board members filed out in a daze, leaving Dave to consider his dwindling career options.

Tex hurried out of the room and headed down the corridor to the elevator. He pressed the call button then waited. As he stood there he noticed something black on the floor that looked like a broken stick. He picked it up and threw it into the chromium-plated garbage can. Those cleaners are getting slack, thought Tex.

The elevator arrived to the muted strains of Mozart's Requiem. He made a final inspection of his matching pair of Colts then stepped into the dark void. Inside the shaft the lift was noticeable by its absence. By the time Tex reached the thirteenth floor he was travelling at over eighty miles per hour.

"Yeeeehaaaaahhhh! I'm comin' Lor..." were his last euphoric words before he splattered into the ground.

Later, at his memorial service, it was remarked by those who knew him best that Tex had been a man of devout faith and religious conviction. His gross stupidity was allowed to pass unremarked for fear of offending his trigger-happy relatives.

Part Thirty-Two

An arm and a leg

Inspector Ray Decca sat at a table in *Hotcha Mocha* one evening with his eyes glued to the door. He felt like a fish out of water in café society, but this was where his informant had requested a meeting so he couldn't do much about it. He'd rejected the early advances of the baristas on the grounds that he was waiting for someone, but as the clock ticked relentlessly by, they increasingly looked like they didn't believe him.

Finally, a tall man with stooping gait, a large floppy hat and long beard entered the café and approached his table.

"The red cow is flying tonight," said the stranger.

"Thank God, for that," said Decca. "Have a seat."

"No, I said *the red cow is flying tonight*," repeated the stranger, more emphatically.

"Oh, I see, yes, of course," said Decca, remembering the coded response. "How udderly ridiculous!" he added, looking around him to ensure there were no witnesses to his embarrassment.

The stranger sat in the chair opposite Decca, gesticulated to a waitress behind the counter to join them and removed his hat. He had long white hair, although the beard was clearly false.

"Two coffees, please," said Decca to the waitress, ignoring the proffered menu. He looked intently at the man facing him for a moment.

"Haven't we met somewhere before?" asked Decca.

"Well, it's perfectly possible, of course," began the stranger, "but I don't think it's at all likely."

"I see," said Decca. "So, what should I call you?"

"Mr Smith," said the stranger.

"Right, no names, no pack-drill," said Decca, tapping the side of his nose.

"No, my name's Smith, Harvey Smith," explained the stranger. "Although I'm not in the phone book," he added.

"You said you had some information for me, is that right?" asked Decca.

"Yes, very valuable information," said Mr Smith.

"In my experience, Mr Smith, Harvey, there's no such thing as a free lunch, so what do you want in return?" asked Decca.

"Why, nothing, Inspector. Surely it's my duty as a law abiding citizen to keep the police informed about illegal activities that come to my attention," said Harvey.

"Well, I'm delighted to hear it," said Decca, relieved.

"Besides, it's always useful to have a friend in high places," added Harvey, cryptically.

Their coffees arrived and Decca picked up the bill. He glanced at it casually.

"Twenty quid for two coffees!" he spluttered, feeling as though he'd received a blow to the solar plexus. He wondered briefly if he could find a disguise; perhaps even borrow Harvey's false beard, and leg it out of the toilet window, but then remembered he was an Inspector in the Metropolitan police. At least he'd been right about the free lunch.

"So, what did you come here to tell me?" asked Decca.

"You have in your custody a certain dangerous criminal," began Harvey.

Decca smiled. "We've got loads of the buggers," he said, "you didn't drag me here just to tell me that, surely?"

"Please," said Harvey, "let me finish. The criminal in question masquerades under the name of James Bolton."

"Yeah, we picked him up at Stonehenge recently, what of him?" asked Decca.

"His real name is Karl Bielefeld and he's the Head of Operations for the Red Square," explained Harvey. "At various times he's been a double, triple and even quadruple agent for the Square, then the Triangle and then the Square again. He'll try to confuse you with his hard luck stories about being the assistant to a failed magician, but believe me, he's a ruthless killer. He arranged all of the recent spate of magician killings in person, although he frequently works with a coloured lady called Ruby Murray."

"I see, well that's all very interesting, of course, but what evidence do you have?" asked Decca.

"I'll send you a file through the mail, inspector, with all the evidence you need to put him away for life," said Harvey.

"Excellent, excellent, Mr Smith. I look forward to receiving it. Incidentally, why didn't you bring it with you tonight?"

"Just a little security precaution, you understand," said Harvey.

"I see," said Decca. "Just one more question: what do you know about something called a *Quark* bomb? It came up in conversation when we were interviewing some suspects," said Decca.

"Ah, yes, the Quark bomb," said Harvey. "I came to the conclusion that it was an elaborate hoax," he added. "You see, the Square's resurgence was funded by selling a mythical explosive device, the Quark bomb, to a bunch of religious fanatics who wanted to blow up the world. The Red Square sold them a silver box containing some sophisticated communications and voice recognition software but they weren't about to blow themselves up, were they? Not even for a few million quid," concluded Harvey.

"No, of course not," said Inspector Decca. Only a fool would have thought otherwise.

They shook hands and Harvey disappeared into the night, leaving Decca to struggle up to the till with a heavy heart to settle the bill.

Part Thirty-Three

A short walk to freedom

It was 11.45 pm on New Year's Eve. Hymie lay scratching himself on the sofa in Mike's apartment with the television blaring in the background. Crowds of people were having immense fun doing silly things in Picadilly and Times Square; some things never changed. He imagined how they'd all feel if they knew how perilously close they'd come to being sucked into a black hole. Probably none of them would believe it, and he couldn't really blame them for he didn't quite believe it himself. Probably some of them would blame *him* for depriving them of a new experience. You could never please everyone, that was why so many people ended up just trying to please themselves but it didn't have much to commend it as a way of life.

Mike was asleep and snoring in his armchair after consuming a dozen beers and a whole ham.

"Oh well, Mike, another year's about to end and what do we have to show for it?" said Hymie. "A few empty beer bottles and the same old crap on the telly. Next year I'm going abroad; somewhere warm and inviting where the women are friendly and the booze is cheap, or vice versa."

"Get lost! I never touched your stinkin' diary!" shouted Mike, in his sleep.

"What the hell are you on about, Murphy?" asked Hymie, resisting the urge to throw something hard at his somnolent buddy.

"I dunno what station it was at," said Mike "but it was definitely a Class 56."

"My God, Mike, I never had you down as a closet train-spotter," said Hymie in mock horror. He struggled to his feet and put on the outsized raincoat that Mike had left draped over the bannister. He needed some fresh air to clear his head and take away the corrosive sense of hopelessness that always afflicted him at that time of year.

Outside on the street it was raining. Hymie turned up his collar, put his hands in his pockets and simply walked. What was his life all about? he wondered. Was it all about finding someone special to share his time and energies with or just about keeping going? He had been so sure that Ruby was *the one* that he couldn't switch off his feelings for her just because she'd turned out to be some kind of terrorist nutter. Even giving him a bomb for Christmas had seemingly been well intentioned. Certainly no one had ever given him anything so valuable before.

He laughed at the thought of such a strange love token and at his own ability to twist the truth to justify her actions, but soon found himself crying in the rain. It didn't matter that it was a cliché, it helped release him from the fundamental sense of loss he'd never managed to express. How else could he reconcile himself to carrying on as normal with his shattered dreams of love and happiness heaped up on all sides? Had she loved him? Would he ever know? In the cold light of day, did it really matter? Were love and happiness just illusions that offered relief for a while from the pain and tedium of existence? And why was he so hung up on the thought that there must be more to life than this?

The rain was pelting down harder now and as Hymie stood beneath a streetlamp offering no shelter and precious little light, the hostility of the elements seemed to pummel him out of his gloom. With an effort of will, he drew back from the emotional precipice of despair and began to focus on the facts that were his stock in trade. Mike and he had saved the world. Few people could claim as much. The Quark bomb was even now sitting de-activated in a bucket of soapy water at 792A Finchley Road. They'd stopped a criminal gang from murdering their rivals and they'd helped the police to catch the bad guys. As for the money, he still had that blank cheque from the insurance company somewhere and they couldn't complain too much if he filled it out for a few hundred thousand quid to tide them over. When you thought about it like that, life didn't get much better. In the distance, Hymie could see and hear Barnet council's entire annual fireworks budget going up in flames. Those guys had the right idea; so what if it *was* raining? He couldn't have been happier if he'd been sipping margaritas on Copacabana beach.